UNCHARTED

UNCHARTED

JON GOWER

Gomer

To Sarah with all my love

Published in Wales in 2010 by
Gomer Press, Llandysul, Ceredigion, SA44 4JL

ISBN 978 1 84851 209 2

A CIP record for this title is available from the British Library.

© Jon Gower, 2010

Jon Gower asserts his moral right under the
Copyright, Designs and Patents Act, 1988
to be identified as author of this work.

This book is published with the financial support of the Welsh Books Council.

Printed and bound in Wales at Gomer Press, Llandysul, Ceredigion

'Every story is a love story . . .'
Robert McLiam Wilson

River City Dreaming

Buenos Aires
34° 35′ S 58° 22′ W

Listen! Like a million small, slippery wet kisses on muddy shore and hard escarpment, on pebble beach and marshy reaches, the enormous river meets the land and sings to it, a song of love, water to earth. It is a polyphonic symphony with a chorus of aqueous voices – sucking seductions, rippling percussion, and millions of swamp frogs looking for a wet date. This is the river song. *Canción del Río*.

Her voice tonight is shored up by huge volumes joining the headwater as an eely legion of silver tributaries bring down Andean snow-melt and rainforest deluge. It is a jaguar sound, a deep subsonic snarl carried from the heart of the jungle – a satisfied sound of imponderable power, as if that cat has wrapped its muscles around a kill. A devil's smile of moonlight glint on ivory fangs.

Riparian tree branches reach like birds' feet to caress the black fur of water – fur that is the epitome of blackness, attended by the contented cat purr of wavelets lapping.

But there are other songs on the breeze as well, on a gentle breeze that carries a perfumed drift from jacarandas, and seduces legions of moths out of their beds.

If you listen carefully you can hear the faint sound of children crying, down in La Boca where the barrios are filled with all human misery and from beyond there, even, from those places in the city where even rags and cardboard are scarce commodities and life is as tough as can be. Little wonder they cry constantly, an incessant wailing like professional keeners. Children without food, toys, parents even, who cry to try to forget the famine knot in the guts, not whinge about it. These are kids who subsist on scraps; whose lives are momentary, passing events.

The river's sub-song is the tympanic thrum of diesel engines, pistoning as huge freight ships heave into harbour after titanic journeys though the tempests of the South Atlantic, where even the seabirds – the black-browed albatrosses and the Manx shearwaters – are driven mad by the wind. Turbines groan in the enormous iron hulks – thrump, thrump, thrump – as the tugboats bring them into safe harbour.

Listen carefully, hush your very heart and you can hear a broken syntax of fractured conversation – partial sentences, snipped phrases – as you tune in to drifts of dream, snag them like wool on wire. In this city there are no secrets. They drift in the air, like spores or moth scales. Musical moth scales. A dust of dreams.

So assemble the fragments of a city's dreaming – hopes mingled with desire, fears expressed in galloping nightmares – as the river song lifts and veers, over dreary buildings and civic splendour, back out over the marshes and widening then over beaches and soft promontories, over ibis haunt and soft shore. Here are creeks and channels that give this place its shape, and offer both rhythm and character to its people. They are the *porteños*, the people of this port, and there is an open door and ready welcome for anyone who disembarks here. Come on in.

This, then, is the city's sustenance, this river that flows inexorably on. It can be destructive too, and moody, but mainly it brings mineral nurture and fish aplenty. It gives skinny-dipping legions of children escape from the oppression of summer heat, as the great elegant mass of water gravitates to the sea. Elegant as tango. Forever tango.

> How much I want to cry
> In this grey afternoon
> In its peal
> The rain speaks of you.
> It's the remorse of knowing
> That it is my fault that I'll never,
> Love . . . never see you again.
> My closed eyes
> See you same as yesterday;
> Trembling, pleading
> For my love again . . .
> Today your voice comes back to me,
> In this grey afternoon.

And the old couple, Horacio and Flavia Trucco dance to this song in their apartment full of dust. Their legs, though pipe-cleaner thin, are as strong as those of a prima ballerina, and their heads held as high as Andalusian royalty. They are the King and Queen of this dance.

The ancient gramophone dissipates Gardel's voice through the room. This was the tender tenor who died too early, even though his voice, a reedy, silver trumpet, will

9

persist through vinyl, acetate, on MP3 and in living memory for as long as the Andes rise above the cordillera. They say it is impossible to understand the sadness of this city without understanding the emptiness and pain that underscore the tangos. And Gardel makes it all clear, exemplary. He makes that sadness explicit, unbearable.

Sometimes, in bright-light days, the mud on the riverbank can look like freshly-cut liver, gigantic butchery. The white egrets flash in the sun as if there is a secret semaphore in their feathers. Away in the north the greenery of Uruguay is a thick charcoal line under a sky which threatens a terrible rain, punctuated by flashes of nervy lightning.

But tonight the river is nothing more than a shimmer of light under the moon, with the occasional tiny 'blip' as indigent fish rise slowly to suck a fly. And a miniature symphony of tree frogs strikes up, making music – they are a lovelorn chorus for the dark, harmonizing a hoarse psalm to the night.

This is the River Plate and, like so many rivers, a city has arranged itself around its mouth. Buenos Aires – where the fresh air of its name is now filled with skeins of smog, trillions of diesel particulates that clog the light. But this is a fabulous city – from the frozen music of its regal buildings (some of them would surely dance a gavotte if brought to life) – to the brutalist tenements that mushroomed in the Seventies. The suburbs spread relentlessly, they go on and on as the city swells, as if they want to claim the horizon itself. And the people keep building, encroaching on the pampas with their concrete, an ant-like multitude as diligent as the ants of São Paulo.

But even this city has to sleep and it's always late in the day when somnolence settles, when the city's energies ebb, when the midnight bells have sounded their long echoes, late at night, when the river's song quietens to a gentle lapping against pilings, a shirr of water against the shore.

But the city doesn't stop working. It's just that night brings different work. The men in the bakery, who look like ghosts under their dustings of flour, suffer from ailments that would be comical, were it not for the fact they were so deadly. Yellow bread lung. Yeast fever, which can erase a worker from the staff list in just three days. Seventy-six hours from the first sprinkling of blood on the handkerchief to death's door, diagnosis to departure lounge. A thick line through a name in the staff ledger, an advert for a new bakery assistant the day after the funeral. Life moves on.

The gas station assistants read cheap novellas even as they ponder whether this will be the night someone comes to make a cash withdrawal at the end of a shotgun barrel. Robbery is epidemic. Assault is endemic. Battery the same.

Just a week ago an eminent literary critic, with a much respected weekly commentary section in *La Nación*, was killed in one of the petrol joints on Avenida 9 de Julio for criticizing the manner in which the robbers were going about their business. His last words before shuffling off this mortal coil were, 'Why are you parodying old B-movies when you could be inventing your own hard men argot, appropriating language to your own ends just as you appropriate the cash, gentlemen?' The bad guys, who must have favoured a different intellectual school, sided with the counter-argument. Ba-bam! One bullet. All his education and learning and some thirty thousand books pondered and remembered blown out in a splattering waterfall from a neat hole in the head. Like a short story, it really was: each red drop a poem.

The robbers are abroad again tonight – working a nocturnal nine to five from dusk to dawn. They are at work as certainly as the motionless nun in her cell. She is hard at work, in her own way, too, whispering her prayers with intensity, knees drawn up close against her straw mattress. She has only the dimming light of one candle to see what there is left of the guttering physical world, even as she reaches up into a higher plane. She knows there is someone listening. She knows she has a conduit to her female God.

'Merciful Señora, bring us comfort and envelop us with your grace. Bless the city as she sleeps. Comfort those who need it the most and give me the strength – if such is your wish – to help them. I know their needs and wants and desire with all my heart to give them succour.'

And then she sings – not a sacred song but an old song about slavery and severed chains, her desiccated voice sustaining a thin melody which carries out over the rooftops to join in the river's arpeggio; its tiny waves in quietest counterpoint to the dissipating voice.

And she is just one of those singing tonight. It's a choir out there. A nightingale shopkeeper, fine-reeded as an oboe; an owl-poet with a deep timbre bassoon, a transsexual baritone and a desperate lunatic making dog noises, all lifting up their voices in supplication and celebration, or because of insomnia, stomach grumbles, too much red wine or overpowering cheese, night terror or moon worship. Whatever. It makes for a lunar cacophony.

And there will be other prayers too. Hebrew chants. *Tehillim*. And kyries, too. The most beautiful words on earth. Kyrie eleison. Lord have mercy. Be merciful towards us. Be most impossibly merciful.

So listen if you can, if you're not in any hurry, to this song of astonishing variety. Lullaby and blessing. *Lieder* and soundscape. Prayer of praise and penance. Above our many sleeping heads, the various and vital inhabitants of Buenos Aires.

One thing is constant. The river voice. Listen! Listen! It has power, complexity, pollutants, nature in abundance and watery productivity. And so too the lexicon for describing it – how the river looks and behaves in its many moods and seasons. Dark-skinned. Milky-coffee-coloured, or in the vase of this river, these rivers, the colour of *dulce de leche*, that ambrosial food that is both milk and caramel and better than any other food (but don't tell a dentist in this city because they all suffer from depression – the *dulce* is one of the biggest reasons). Argentina is a chart-topper when it comes to dental caries; so many mouths just pocked caves of dental rot, gingival recession fit to take your gums away.

The World Health Organization expresses its concern in heavy, authoritative reports, but sweet-toothedness persists. And the dentists slip further into black dog days. As it happens, one, a literate man with a fine sense of humour – will hang himself this very night – and do so,

13

ironically enough, using a cord made by twisting together a quarter of a mile of dental floss over a three-week period. It's robust enough to take his weight as he topples the chair from under him, to dangle there as his eyes become empty, as his bowels seep.

The warning signs had been there, flashed out with the certainty of egret wings – the tidying of each and every room, the almost daily visits to the bank, the dinner dates with close friends, not one of them sensing the turmoil within, ticked off a mental tally. In that he would have made a great poker player. Not one of them guessed that Hugo Martinez didn't see the world as a projection like Plato's cave, but rather saw its reality as a dungeon filled with huge broken teeth like gravestones, and he wanted out, more than anything.

This is the mental inventory of ways of describing the river the dead dentist Martinez kept in his head:

Lion-maned flow.

An azulejo flow – blue-grey, like horses.

A visual echo of the Argentine flag as it flies above the palaces.

A powder blue, a rare chalk hue.

A flat red plain, a soup of curdling silt.

Water the colour of chocolate.

Green water, laden with duckweeds.

Glistening gunmetal under a harsh sun.

In his notebook, Martinez the depressed dentist had captured the river in all its seasons. Not much good to him now.

14

Chapter 1

Los Libros

Fly over the city, feel how the heat rises from the earth, be amazed by the extravagant expanse of the water below, and the city's concertinaed map, which is spreading its concrete lanes and highrises like a virus. There are the new barrios, built under cover of night by men who ooze desperation like sweat. And that's where the children cry the loudest. La Boca. The river mouth. You've seen it.

Fly like the mythical kingfisher in the story *porteños* tell to their awed children. That halcyon bird, with a bill like a Scottish dirk, a stabbing dagger.

The bird dies after eating a fish that belongs to the King of the Fish – *Oh, He Who Must Be Worshipped!* He is the King of all things finned and gilled and He it is who created a space for them in both dark ocean and desert pool – for the pupfish of the Mojave Desert – yes, there is a fish that lives in the desert – and the coelacanth of ocean trench, for iridescences of herring to scythe through chill seas and herds of seahorses to drift aimlessly with the tide.

The kingfisher resurrects as readily as it will die again, a cycle repeated over and over again. Like the story itself, changed with the retelling. Myth is, after all, only very old gossip. Why don't you fly higher now, enjoy the sweeping air, as it catches in your primary feathers, giving you tilt and control? Your feathers have a diesel sheen, like light on oily water.

And if you swoop through the air and the vapour of thin clouds, and follow the sodium lights of one of the wide *avenidas* that stretch out toward the south and then turn in a tight curve above the extraordinary façade of the oldest bookshop in the country and then bank left above the shop where the old lady makes the most sought-after *empanadas* and then lose height to drift in through the heavy mahogany door of Number 13, Calle Gibson, as if the wood has turned into gossamer, become competely without substance, you can proceed up the stairs and into the first room on the left where you'll see a young boy asleep. He is wearing a velveteen hat on his head – he wears it all the time – even when he is forced to have a bath. On those occasions his mother forcibly removes it even as he howls like a sea lion.

'Washing it, Jaime, that's all I'm doing,' says his mother, always eager to placate the boy. For he is her only, precious son.

Jaime is his only name. He doesn't have a surname because his mother, Esmeralda, who now works in a run-down coffee shop but used to work in much, much worse places, such as the room-by-the-hour flop shops, the hot pillow hotels, doesn't know who the father was and won't give her son any other name than that of her own father by way of forename. She wouldn't know the biological father if he was standing right in front of her. A tear in a condom changed her fate. Anyway, she is tall and handsome and like all mothers, a fabulous heroine.

It is three in the morning and the child has only just come in after a hard night's collecting and packing. He works in concert with other gatherers, gleaning cardboard and paper on the streets, slaving like a Trojan to break down the boxes and get them ready for the bundler who compacts them into big, brown cubes with his antique-looking press. The old guy who does the bundling has outsized arm muscles like Popeye. Jaime compacts the newspaper himself, using twine to shape and contain the piles. His brown arms work quickly, lassoing the papers and pulling them into place with a speed that confounds the eye. The others call him the Monkey and they are very fond of him – he is an effortlessly happy worker and sings with gusto as he takes his haul to the flatbed truck, its tyres flattened by the weight. He sings lullabies his grandmother taught him, and songs he's heard breaking through the static on the radio. They give him strength, distract him from the aches in his muscles, these songs evoking the cordilleras, rhythmic hymns to condors and high land, tales of love, both lost and won, though mainly lost.

His mother has left for work by the time he gets up but she has covered a full plate of leftover pastries from the café to protect them from flies. She always gets goods for nothing. Even though Jaime eats industrial amounts of them there is little danger of his growing fat, as he works so hard, burning off calories in the furnace of his effort.

In the café Esmeralda sells deep-fried *empanadas* to men who are exhausted after working night shifts in the factories and entirely spent after working illegally long hours behind the wheels of taxicabs. So tired are they that some find it a strain to chew the pastries, even, with their rich mix of beef, currants and eggs, their flavour barely registering. The men's eyes are like dead fish as they eat, for they are licked by life, worked over by it and the testing strain of working two or three jobs to make ends meet. Ever since the peso was devalued living has been hard. But she knows the men will be in tomorrow and every day afterwards, looking increasingly exhausted and zombified.

Esmeralda works eighteen-hour days herself and she'll often double up as short-order cook as well as waitress: she is always ready with her smile, and popular because of it. Some of the men flirt with her, in that pathetic way that lonely men have, or in that sly way married men develop, now that their wives have put on weight or grown too familiar. Love between a man and woman is so fragile, like the papery wrap of a butterfly cocoon: that between a mother and child so invincible. The flirty men try out all their lines:

– Are you free tonight – or will it cost?

– Here's 20 centavos – phone your mother to say you won't be coming home tonight.

She has heard them all by now, every pick up line known to pathetic man, some sharp, some dumb, some chance.

– You're the one.

The words are traps for the unwary. Sometimes she goes next door to the bar called El Faro for a brandy with one of the men before turning for home. One of them is 'El Gato', 'the cat', and no one is exactly sure why he's been given this name, though it's probably explained by the way his body moves, a slinkiness in his manner. His

18

real name is Manuelito and Esmeralda loves the way his eyes engage the world around him, drawing it in, not content with just reflecting it. She enjoys his self-confident demeanour. She likes his voice, too, which carries the cragginess of his mountain childhood in the hard consonants that sound like rock being chipped with a mandrill. And the long 'o' he uses, like the sound of red-backed hawk wheeling and crying over the highlands.

He also has a stammer, which makes him seem weak, when in fact he is anything but. Manuelito was the only man who didn't presume that her acceptance of a drink was a passport to her bedroom. He was blessed with an old style chivalry and that was why she went to bed with him, that first time. That eventual first time. After he'd told her about the dream, over a third brandy, one evening when he realized that there was something beautiful accreting around them. His dream had recurred so many times he'd lost count.

He was riding a horse in the Andean foothills, the muscular land rising jagged and rocky-toothed around and above him, with eroded dragon shapes mutating into wind-sculpted pillars and mesas like the ones in Arizona. He was carrying a letter for a hermit who lived way up in a hut that had neither electricity nor water. It's best to say even this early in the account of the dream – lest it appear that it is something straight out of the Brothers Grimm – that the hermit was not a poor man. In fact, he was the son of a wealthy merchant banker from London, who was poised to inherit a fortune one of these days. The letters Manuelito carried in his extraordinarily detailed dream were sent from the only private post office in Britain, other than the Queen's own postal service, the really private one, with trained falcons and tiny parchments on chains. So a tweedy lady in a gentlemen's club in Pall Mall had forwarded the letter. Details, details.

Manuelito was wearing a red felt hat and had a heavy mantle of alpaca wool draped around his shoulders. His palomino was the nervous sort of steed, taking hesitant steps across the scree. He remembered all the detail: it was the sort of dream a dreamer pays attention to, even in the murkily indistinct realm of the subconscious. The detail was graphic, like a car maintenance manual.

The horse was wary as it breasted through groves of thorn in the dry valley, even as Manuelito hacked and slashed his way through, aiming to win through to the other side of the riven gulch within the hour. A yellow-and-black snake slid in front of them and curled to defend itself, rearing and uttering a chilling hiss from a devilish head before being absorbed by leaf dapple. The air was thin and the horse breathed stertorously from fear and lack of oxygen, its lungs beating like bellows.

In the distance the mountains were translucent blue, a solid sea of rock. As he slowly gained on them Manuelito could see that they were actually blue, a geological feature rather than a trick of the light.

When he arrived at the hut the hermit wasn't there, but the door was ajar so Manuelito hesitated for an instant, then went inside. He placed the letter on the table and was about to leave, so he could be back home before nightfall, but instead he decided to rest for a few minutes on the one chair. He was almost instantly asleep. He woke up to see a curious apparition – a hat and scarf floating in the middle of the room – and even though there is usually nothing frightening about hats and scarves, this particular hat and scarf did put the fear of God, or something, into him. Scared to the marrow, he started to recite a fractured mantra made of remembered bits of catechism, scripture readings, the Lord's Prayer and as if by way of reply the clothes disappeared, dematerialized as if they had never, ever been there.

Esmeralda had been listening intently to every word uttered by the man with magnetic eyes, and her attention had been riveted by the last part of the dream as she herself had had a disturbingly similar dream about a hat and scarf, floating in mid-air, threateningly! She almost failed to get the words out to explain. Even listening to his version had brought the night terrors flooding back. When he offered his hand by way of comfort she took it with alacrity before leaning her body against his.

Now, if Satan himself had appeared to them, or a gigantic serpent with silver eyes and hypodermic fangs, or some such horror, it would have made more sense somehow, but a hat and scarf! What was it about those items of clothing, and even more intriguingly, they themselves that they should have this dream in common?

In his room – he happened to live next door but one to the bar and they got there in less than two minutes – they shared a large class of aguardiente of some kind, the neat alcohol singeing their lips. Then, without any seeming cue, they drew close and their bodies began to furl and coil, and

21

clothes were shucked, tongue tasted tongue. She wriggled out of her black work dress and he took off his solid work boots and the two of them were laughing at the gay abandon of it and there was no embarrassment about it. As she sat on top of him, felt him grow in her most intimate embrace, she felt as if she'd always known him and that these moments were inevitable, preordained, that they could never be taken away. They both moved in time to an inner music. United in rhythm, harmonious in movement, they moved onwards as their bodies sweated towards an exultant release.

Then, in a movie moment, Manuelito lit a cigarette and started talking nonsense, a homely pillow talk that made her feel comfortable and safe. He even spoke about the weather, as her insides tingled and the aroma of tobacco lulled her to sleep, laughing quietly as she drifted. The weather!

Without words, he cradled her beneath his arm and pulled her in as if he wanted their bodies to meld as one. She nestled in a cave of warmth, where she wanted to be.

Jaime is too tired to concentrate in school – even though the geography lesson is one of his favourites and the American lady, who struggles to keep order, is both prim and funny. She comes from a city of which he'd never heard, even though Miss Lucy says it's the place from which the best hip hop in the known universe comes. He isn't keen on the music but many of his friends like it because it's what they watch on TV. She plays something by a band called 'The Coup' through her iPod deck almost immediately after she's introduced herself, explaining how they'll be learning about a lot of things through music, even maths, which she avers is a sort of music. Playing the songs is a nice gesture. And he covets the player, as do all the other kids in class. If they own one they can be like the children on television. They take it in turns to plug in the little white earpieces and feel the heft of the box on the palms of their hands.

Jaime's friend Jorge isn't in school today as he's had an accident in the workshop where he cuts flowers ready for packing. Some days his hands bleed – as do those of his friends who work in a room which is dim from only having two light bulbs. The wire that binds the carnations is cruel to young hands.

Sleep threatens to envelop Jaime: the American teacher's descriptions of the world flow into a stream of meaningless patter, jumbled with the names of countries, and Jaime fights the encroaching sleep as if it is fire, trying to beat it back, but the waves are relentless. Even though she is talking about places he burns with desire to see – the dry deserts of Chile, the endangered virgin forests of Brazil, the impenetrable Gran Chaco of Paraguay – the facts and images merge and tumble. A train runs through a huge expanse of thorn where smugglers act as modern pirates. He sees skulls and crossbones on their Toyota Land Cruisers. Waterfalls fail to drown out the sound of startled parakeets. A scarlet macaw, hit by an arrow from an Amazonian rifle, explodes in a red supernova of feathers. The small boy's head leans ever forwards as the litany of names flows together: 'Santiagoatacamachubutpatagonia-

cordobacordilleratierradelfuegothelandoffireattheendofthe
world . . .

'Jaime!'

The teacher's voice sounds as if it's muffled by cotton wool, all dreamy, faraway.

Insistent rain everywhere and everything looks dank. Horacio and Flavia are wearing their best clothes. He is dressed tidily in a suit normally only aired at funerals nowadays and she is garbed in a fur coat her grandmother bought from a fur trader in Northern California's Russian River at the turn of the century, wearing it all the way south as she rode on the early railroads and on tired nags. What started as a look of faded grandeur had become tatterdemalion by the time she reached home but she still wears it when she can, because this is her American coat and she has worn it on long treks and it has kept her warm in the mountains and at night. The scent of that gargantuan journey sticks to the pelt so that it is a sort of specimen case. The dust of dead insects, the dampness of a canvas tent, the tang of the long sea journey, the zip of juniper scent.

They walk regally to the end of the street, where they hail a cab. This will be Horacio's first time in a taxi, but today warrants the cost. As the car drives through the rain-slickened streets Horacio counts out his money nervously. The numbers on the meter turn at an alarming rate so that he hardly looks out the window. Today the doctor will give his wife the results of the tests. Her cancer is now established, a thing of appetite. She grows weaker by the day. The pallor of her skin makes her shine in the dark.

Some nights, as they dance to the old tunes – Troello coaxing rich sounds from the bandoneón, or Pugliese caressing the keyboard as if he was outlining his first lover's hips – Horacio will chance upon his wife's ribs, held in a compacting cage of flesh. He can feel, with his fingertips, her heart beating, its pulse and fear, its rhythm and presence. It beats whirringly, like a hummingbird, as if it could fly away from here, out into the night.

Horacio knows she feels he suffocates her sometimes, for even love can asphyxiate. But all he wants is to be near her, to be next to her. He watches the city go past, registering no detail, his mind active with schemes to bring his wife some comfort.

The taxi driver comes from Armenia and has a voice treacly with nicotine. He drives like a madman among all the other mad people. This is an open-air asylum with everyone licensed to kill, as they rush home to meet the nurse with her trolley of medicines. Driving in Buenos Aires first requires a stiff drink, or Librium if you're heading out to the airport.

Señor and Señora Trocca sit like stone images, his counting done, her mind in a dark place. Over the city flash lightning flickers, with attendant thunder: percussive cracking to break the fug.

They know the doctor well and have been visiting his clinic for half a century. He has an assured way of dealing with his patients, a confidence that can make some of them feel better straight away. He explains things in a way that

25

is painstakingly clear, and always offers a coffee or brandy. He has always, always read the notes before the patient comes in, so that they never have to wait in uneasy silence. His coat is white and his breath is often saturated with brandy, but today he is as sober as can be, as he knows Señora Trocca's path leads into the dark woods. He wishes he could go with her, be her guide past the stumps of fallen trees and the liana overhangs, to show her how to skirt the dark places. But that is not the way. The doctor imagines how her husband will take the news, how he will be smithereened by it.

'Would you care for a drink?' asks the doctor, gesturing towards both kettle and bottle.

'No thank you,' answer the couple, their voices in unison.

The doctor upholds his own standards and doesn't beat about the bush.

'I cannot explain things better than to tell you in terms of time. Señora Trocca, I'm so very sorry. You only have a fortnight left to you, I'm afraid. We can help you deal with the pain but the cancer is racing through your body and raging in vital organs. I have only one suggestion. Would you now consider going into the hospital, where at least we can keep you comfortable?'

In a voice that is disarmingly confident and full, the old lady refuses, insisting that she wants to be with her husband during all the time that remains to them and says, unequivocally, that it is her wish to die in her own bed. The doctor counters by saying that Horacio can be with her all the time in the hospital but there is a determined look in the dark currant eyes of the dying woman which suggests that any argument he marshalls will be futile in the extreme. He knows this kind of determination: her generation had to be determined to survive.

The two old people bow as they leave – deep bows like Japanese worshippers in the temple of Kiyomizu-dera in Kyoto, even though this pair have never left their native city, or even met someone from Japan. It is an unusual gesture. The ancient lovers leave with heads held high, as usual.

Outside, the terror of what they've been told threatens to dismantle them. They stand outside a flower shop like pieces in a statuary. Dread turns their skin into marble.

'I'll be with you until the world ends. Until the sun falls from the sky, my love, my beautiful bride.'

He runs out of clichés. Nearly.

'You are the one.'

That night they go to L'Aventura for dinner – a down-at-heel restaurant that has seen better days. The grey wallpaper peels like grim festoons from the damp walls. The chairs are held together by electrical tape. The men who serve here are old – courteous zombies in crisp white shirts with time-crenellated collars and sober black ties. But they are also resourceful old men, crafty in the way they make sure the old couples who dine here feel they are in a special place on a blessed evening. How so? Even though there are only two elements to the set meal – meat and vegetables and the ubiquitous caramel flan – the old boys always ask, 'Have the señoras chosen?' – and by dint of this single question they manage to keep their customers' geriatric fantasies intact. They make the menu seem much longer, help maintain the dignity of old people.

As she picks at her flan Flavia tells Horacio that she will love him after she is dead. The old man's body shudders with emotion and his eyes gush cataracts of tears.

'It's true,' says the old woman, who has volunteered to learn a special code, a specific list of numbers, that as been devised by mathematicians at the University of Buenos Aires. They have a scheme to test communication with the dead, and if she can successfully communicate the list to them after she has passed then the scientists will have bridged the awful chasm. The numbers have been generated by a computer and will be known only to a computer operator and to her. She cannot tell him what they are but she wants him to be alert, on the lookout for them.

She tells him more about the nature of the experiment and how the scientists have been working with colleagues in Canada and Arizona, studying the moment of death and its many consequences.

'And do people actually get in touch from the other side?' Horacio asks.

'Not yet, Horacio.'

He's been listening to her without understanding everything she says. His spoon sits on the plate for he has no appetite. He doesn't want a single thing, other than to keep his wife by his side.

Abélard and Eloise. Antony and Cleopatra. Adam and Eve. Horacio and Flavia.

One night, as Jaime worked on the streets in one of the eastern suburbs of the city, a tall woman came out of a Chilean restaurant called Tres Estrellas and paid him a great deal of attention. He was ripping the cardboard with gusto and applying as much pressure to it as he could, before handing it to one of the men with leather aprons. The bundles were then loaded on a cart.

The stranger looked at him for some minutes, without the usual embarrassment with which people in grand clothes normally caught sight of him, averting their eyes as quickly as they could. Most of them walk swiftly by. Then the woman walked up to the principal baler and asked how she could contact the boy the next day, to discuss business. That flummoxed the man. Who on earth uses the word 'business' with owlish workers who keep night hours and are dressed worse than derelicts, in fact are only one grade up from absolute dereliction? And what sort of business? But the woman had a kind, heart-shaped face, so Juan the baler gave her Jaime's uncle's address, suggesting that would be the best way. *He keeps a shop over in Buedo and owns a phone. Yes, definitely the best way to contact the boy.*

Jaime eavesdropped, even though he had barely an inkling of what was going on. Yet he was mature enough to know – for he lives in a world where kids have to accelerate through to the point where they do know such things – that something big was afoot. The woman smelled of geranium and lemon drops. Her hair shone like coal under the streetlights.

The woman's name is Phyllida Gellhorn and she is forty-eight and has a long history of working with Non Governmental Organisations in as many countries as you can shake a stick at. She's a Canadian who has lived longer in Argentina than she has in North America. By now she speaks the patois of the *porteño* to such an extent that she has lost the staccato pace of speech that went with living in cities such as Oakland and Minneapolis, where she was a probing reporter with the best of them.

Now she works as a publisher specialising in children's books and especially *Las Aventuras del Gato Verde*, which is the sort of runaway success story all publishers dream about. It's a simple tale about a cat which falls into a vat of green paint, so that it leaves its paw prints everywhere, all over town, all over the page, and because this is a kids' book, the paint never dries. There is green splash all around the mousehole where the cat, called simply Green Cat, *El Gato Verde*, spends an hour each and every day, just watching. There is paint all across the garden and down the alleyway where every day Green Cat visits its friend Tito. And, of course, there is plenty of evidence when something goes wrong, which it often does, because we're talking about Green Cat, an animal happily disposed to adventure.

Phyllida Gellhorn has just had an idea, or perhaps something bigger than a mere idea: she is awash with a gigantic brain wave, the sort of idea that comes as a deluge and changes everything in its wake. And the idea has arrived pretty much fully formed. Crashed in.

She has an image of a book in her head: a book that has cardboard covers and pages made of recycled paper, a bit like the fancy notebooks you see in some of the upscale stationery shops. But her book is different in that there are lots and lots of them and they are cheap as can be and they are run off by the tens of thousands. As she drives home she talks nineteen to the dozen to her husband but between his poor hearing and the number of cocktails he has poured down his neck, he is none too astute. Besides, his wife's word are galloping along in the most thoroughbred manner. He can't keep up.

When Jaime gets home that evening, he stops, as he always does, to leave a small pile of paper outside the door of the old couple that live downstairs. He hardly ever sees either of them but there is always music creeping out under the door – those old songs that can slice the heart in two. Jaime loves them and will often linger to learn a melody as it seeps through the crack. If he has enough time he'll squat on his haunches and listen carefully, committing the tunes to memory, so that he can sing them to himself as he works.

After they hear the boy's footsteps turning the corner of the stairs and then the sound of the upstairs fire door opening, Horacio steps outside gingerly and picks up the papers. He then carries them into the cramped dining room, where he has been busy cutting up thousands of little strips of paper, which he then glues on to the evolving frame of his creation. The frame itself is also made of paper, but with each successive generation of stuck-on paper it grows in strength. It is also a fractured, dislocated narrative: tales of this city, accounts of this nation.

31

Football headlines bisect news of murders laid over political commentary and entertainment gossip. Strips of *La Nación* over ribbons of the same length and width cut from the *Buenos Aires Herald*. Gradually its shape begins to form and he strengthens the front, side and back. He keeps on building, using every delivery of newspapers to build up the shape of the thing, so that lines from *La Prensa* and *Clarín, La Razón* and *La Capital* cross and blur and there are now thousands of narratives crisscrossing in crazy abandon, something like the higgledy-piggledy story of the city itself, built partly from Chinese whispers and partly from remembered history. Palimpsest on palimpsest. There are headlines and bylines, paragraphs of print and columns of argument: how the first penguins of spring landed on the coast of Chubut with almost clockwork precision, marking the season as surely as swallows in Europe (page 12 of *El Cronista*); the madcap railings and anti George Bush ravings of Chavez 'the pinko oil baron', which attracted the attention of *Ámbito Financiero*; a killing in San Telmo and in the Claramente and in a few other places in a monthly crime round-up; an oil strike in Patagonia; a rare wine harvest delights makers from Cordoba to Mendoza . . . cellar carefully and your grandchildren will be able to toast your wisdom. Every story, no matter how well written, and no matter how thorough the research, is turned into precise squares and meticulous rectangles as Horacio's sharp scissors and shaky hands advance their work. More bits of paper. *Bistec*, 24 pesos only, another murder, a new opinion poll, half a story here, half a story there. Eight more inches of news, some adverts on top, as his creation finally takes shape . . .

The first time Jaime and Manuelito meet is far from being a success. Esmeralda has asked the boy to behave, even though she knows he is at heart a really well-behaved kid. But he is also independent, and this quality has created the need in him to do fatherly things in the absence of a father. Despite his bantam size there is a touch of the alpha male about him, and friction between him and other men is inevitable, especially a man who has started to claim too much of his mother's time which Jamie finds rare enough to begin with. In another time, in another place, they would already be fighting with knives, the blades startling, the blood inevitable.

For this introduction his mother has chosen a pizzeria where Jaime always goes on his birthday (he likes the food there so much he has been known to go through their garbage cans looking for crusts and uneaten food at other times of the year). She thinks this might make him view the evening as a treat of some kind. In fact he sees it as his world being invaded, everything being overturned. In his fanciful young mind he sees it as akin to a wild tribe rushing into his village and razing all the straw huts to the ground, raping the women and, well, even the animals aren't safe from this lot. Manuelito makes him angry beyond words, and as the man stammers he wishes he could twist and yank that stupid tongue out of his mouth. What does his mother see in this cretin, this yammering moron?

33

'You . . . you . . . enjoy school – according to your mother.'

Manuelito's stammer intensifies with the pressure of the situation. Jaime glowers at his mother.

'You had no right to talk to this . . . stranger about what I do or do not do in school . . .'

He spits out the words in a spray of spittle. They have pretty much the same effect on Manuelito, who forces a brave and fixed smile. He is willing to persist in his efforts with the lad, not only because he adores Jaime's mother but because the boy works like a Trojan, placing a brown envelope of cash on the table every Friday night, not that a street boy earns anything like he should for the hours and the daunting effort. He doesn't keep so much as a centavo for himself: his mother doles out pocket money by way of teaching him prudence.

Over their very late breakfast the old couple are discussing euthanasia and how the local soccer team, Boca Juniors did in the local derby against the River Plate. Not very well. The two disparate subjects meld seamlessly. The old man, pouring orange juice, says he knows someone who could get them half a syringeful of liquid that would work very swiftly and without pain (he has one eye on the other half of the liquid for himself, for later) even though he doesn't admit that the friend is, in fact, their doctor, who had waylaid him on the way to the tienda. The partisan voice on the radio blames the scoreline on the referee who clearly had mislaid both seeing dog and white stick.

It takes them a full half-hour to get dressed in their

dancing clothes. She breathes heavily now, and every movement is a grave effort. Her husband places the needle on one of their favourite records, one of Carlos Cesar Lenzi's songs – 'A Media Luz' – which crackles through the air in the appropriate half-light. And as the words swirl elegantly around the room, the two begin to move in stately progress, their torsos stiff, their heads near motionless, although their legs move almost gymnastically. From the waist up the tango is seemingly effortless, disdainful of movement, but the legs, well, the legs have it. Half the body still and half in constant and complicated motion. She hardly looks at him: he hardly looks at her, and he would find it very hard to look at her, so tenderly does he love his dying wife who has been all to him for so many years. Lenzi steers them around . . .

Corrientes 348,
Second floor, elevator
There are neither doormen nor neighbours.
Inside, cocktail and love.
Loft furnished in maple:
Piano, rug and night lamp,
A telephone that answers,
A phonograph that cries
Old tangos of my flower
And a porcelain cat
That can't mew the love.

And the two hold on to each other, hold on for very life. They feel each other's presence, utterly as one in their movements, and for a fleeting moment their eyes meet and it is as if it's the first time – him carrying a box of shoes across Estados Unidos and her carrying a small tissue of flowers to give to her violin teacher after passing the exam, and as she dances with happiness along the pavement she fails to see the road mender's hole into which she stumbles, and in that memory of the first time he can see through all the years that intervene to the bright moment when her eyes – startled and clear – looked into his as he offered her a gallant hand, lifting her and helping her back on her feet.

Wearied now, Horacio's feet snag on the carpet, his wife too brave to show that she cannot dance much longer. She gives him this gift, this last dance. She sees a dapper, younger version of her husband lift some yellow roses and place them back in their cone of paper, a casual but treasured memory. He sees how yellow her skin is, how jaundice-pallid, like the daylight seeping from the sky outside. His wife's liver under siege. His wife's kidneys are under attack. A last dance, perhaps. And she dances with impossible precision all the way through the next stanza, her memory for the sway of notes intact, even if her body is failing.

> And everything at half-light
> That love is a sorcerer . . .
> At half-light the kisses . . .
> At half-light the two of us . . .
> And all at half-light . . .
> Interior twilight . . .
> What soft velvet
> The half-light of love . . .

In a room filled with ornate and heavy colonial architecture, with views over the Plaza Mayor and the cathedral, Phyllida is making her case. The table seats twenty monied men, and she is here to appeal to business sense and harry their consciences.

'Gentlemen. I want to talk to you about an opportunity to give Argentina pride in itself and to give yourselves pride in your actions.'

This inclusivity right at the outset was textbook stuff, as was the rivalry she was about to engage . . .

'We will be seen as so unlike our uncivilized neighbour – where the police hunt down children of the streets and shoot them dead, where venal talk of money drowns out all poetry. There are places where kids are chased right through the *favelas* and gunned down like dogs in front of their mothers. We, the literate, Argentine people want even the poorest children to be cultured, to have a chance of beauty in their lives. And this is why I'm proposing The Great Library of Argentina, which will see all our classics, modern and old – in fact the whole glorious canon of our literature made available to all, on paper picked up from the streets and then recycled and bound between cardboard covers, using cardboard some of our poorest street urchins have gathered as they slave away while many of us sleep.'

'But doesn't this insult our great writers such as Cortázar and Borges, who deserve to be bound in leather, with their names in gold lettering on the spines? Their work shouldn't be found in a cardboard sandwich,' challenges a man with a face as florid as a fuschia flower.

'Not so, sir. Quite the reverse. Every contemporary author worth his or her salt has signed a petition backing this idea to the hilt. And were Cortázar alive today I'm pretty sure he'd have added his signature, in blood if need be. This is a way of getting a whole nation to read books, to regain their birthright.'

And then the masterstroke . . .

'And as I've been suggesting, while our neighbours sully the very idea of innocence and curtail childhood in any meaningful way for hundreds of thousands, I'm sure you'll agree we're a people who love and respect our children, yes we love them and respect the space they need to grow and blossom as individuals, asking only the familiar trinity of them in return – that they love us back, that they keep to the basic rules and work in school – not much to ask when all is said and done. And this will inject equality into the lives of children from Catamarca to Ushuaia, from Formosa to Mendoza, as they all get to read what is rightly theirs – their written heritage. And we shall teach them all to read and by damn, and when we've finished every work of note from Argentina – Centenera to Cortazar, Prado to Puig – then we'll start filling the bookshelves with other great works of the world – Shakespeare, Calvino, Brodsky, Muldoon, Ted Hughes, Elias Canetti, Caradog Prichard and Patrick White.'

She mentions White on purpose, knowing that his name would be unfamiliar to them and this would be unsettling, prey on their minds a little, make them feel ignorant, however temporarily. She loves his *Tree of Man* more than any other book she'd read and had it read it at least eight times. A pure story, Old Testament stuff, about establishing a home in a hard place. She thinks he should be taught here, in this country, where its parable would be taken as documentary.

She is asked to leave the room while the men deliberated her suggestions. They have pot bellies bursting with power. They do not take long to achieve a consensus and soon she was back in the room with them. The director of the Banco Nacional, the one with a pot belly in which you could hide barrels, has a broad smile on his face as he explains that they are of a mind to give every peso asked for, and, furthermore, everyone in the room, in their capacities as employers, will release key staff on secondment, so she will be able to make more money, keep accounts, have marketing know-how, and by dint of these be able to set her sights even higher.

'You are a persuasive lady with considerable reserves of energy,' said the country's most important banker – who would later offer her a place on his board.

'We are maturing as a twenty-first century country,' says a former vice-president, who is keen to hang on the coat-tails of this idea as a means to launch himself a new career. This woman has also sparked a desire in him to write a memoir, something to make it onto a list of the future.

'And if ever the National Bank offers you major league money to go and work for them then the Party would like to say publicly that we would more than match it. We know a national heroine in the making, most certainly,' says another politician.

'And because we're the Banco Nacional, if ever you

make an offer we'll match it, even if we have to have a new print run of banknotes and use up all the purple ink,' retorts the head of the bank. 15 all.

They laugh at that outrageous conceit. This gives Phyllida, who was trembling inside, time to compose herself. She thanks them with all her heart, announcing that she is going to start work that afternoon by trying to contact the little boy who triggered the idea in her mind, imagining that he might be the public face of the project. She has his uncle's number in her little black book, which is about to swell with useful contacts. Phyllida thanks them all for their wisdom, and further for wisdom they will impart to generations as yet unborn.

When she reached the street below she phoned the uncle and asked for the address. Despite a whipping wind that felt as if was flailing in from Patagonia, she decided to walk across the city, which would also help quieten the tremors of excitement that shuddered through her. She deliberately went past the shanty town at the back of the station, where the inhabitants had dug in when the city announced they were going to bulldoze the place, arguing that if they were given a reasonable sum from the future developers of the site they could themselves move up one step in life. She could hear a chorus of kids' voices behind the wall that separated the sprawling camp from the railway tracks.

The shop, when she reached it, was dark, not because it was closed but because the entire stock of second-hand toys was lit by the light of just one candle and even the flame of that seemed to gutter emphysemically. A stuffed

40

baboon, missing one eye, hung from its own mangy arm over the till, which itself looked like a museum piece. The antique till was set theatrically as an island on an aluminium foil pond where flocks of plastic ducks swam. As her eyes adjusted to the gloom she could discern an enormous pile of jigsaws and noted that each box was marked with three sets of numbers. There was the price, then the number of pieces and then the number of pieces the box should contain, so a purchaser could work out precisely how many pieces were missing. She thought someone would have to be very poor indeed to buy a jigsaw without all the pieces, then realized that someone had had to count the pieces – to do the maths. One box contained 1898 pieces out of two thousand. It would look like a wool sock after the moths had finished dining, a puzzle suitable for those with attention deficit disorder. *Start again, why don't you? Oh, don't worry, start again with a different piece.*

'May I help you, señora?' asked a man in a brown shop coat. He had a shock of white hair, which hung luxuriously over his shoulders.

'I'm looking for a young man called Jaime.' Phyllida replied. 'Do you know where I might find him?'

'Oh! You must be the lady who phoned earlier. Now he hasn't done anything wrong – I can vouch for that. He's as honest as the day is long.'

The man burbled his words rather but he was undeniably protective of the boy. Jaime's uncle admired the fact he worked like a robot. His nephew was the sort who could climb up out of the ditch, as his grandmother used to say: he could make something of himself. He really would.

'No. He's not in trouble – I hope quite the opposite. I have a scheme to publish hundreds of thousands of affordable books – most of them affordable because they'll be free, and I'd like him to permit us to take photographs of him to use when we publicize our new library.'

'Why him?' asked the old man, who had no clue what she was talking about.

'Because he's a hard worker . . . and I saw him one night trying to read one of the papers he'd collected. I could see the frustration in his face. And one way to tackle illiteracy is to give people worthwhile things to read, coupled, of course, with the skills to read them.'

'He finds it hard to concentrate in school,' replied the uncle. 'And by the time his mother comes home she's too tired to help him – and she herself finds reading a difficulty . . . But let me say one thing if I may? If you single him out for attention then he'll become a target for other kids. He'll be fighting day and night.

'We'll take care of that. And by the way, would you like to come to work for me yourself? We'll need someone with experience of the retail sector.'

The two old men were drinking coffee and staring meditatively out of the window at the rush of people wearing raincoats and carrying umbrellas, and at the way the wind sent streams of jacaranda petals like confetti down the *avenida*.

'She's weakening by the minute,' said Horacio, his cheeks wet with tears.

'Is it time for me to help you out?' asked the doctor, employing his most professional tone of voice. He had helped a good many people leave this earth ahead of the allotted time, and had done so with a clear conscience. Who would choose to live a life of pain and share that pain with all their family? Not Hippocrates himself, he'd bet.

'I will need your help,' said Horacio. 'But not in the way you suggest. She wants to leave, but doesn't want that coward's drift into the arms of Morpheus, using drugs. But she is ready to leave. Do you have ten minutes to come over to the flat – she's fast asleep at the moment? I have something to show you.'

An old, heavy key turned in an outsized lock and the two men walked ceremoniously up the time-worn marble stairs, past the rows of locked doors and into the flat. It was dark and there was only the sound of Flavia's troubled, bronchitic breaths, the sound of caged budgerigars. With his finger to his lip, Horacio led the doctor to the dining room, where the doctor beheld a boat made entirely out of paper. Using his usual forensic logic, he thought that Horacio had chosen his material deliberately. Suitable for sinking. He noted the shape of the supine figure in the room next door, was intrigued by the care lavished on making the boat's paper sides. He could imagine her sandwiched in the keel. Death by slow drowning – chosen in preference over sleeping tablets or a pillow pressed over a mouth, mercifully applied. He could see it.

'She wants to go on the river for her last journey,' said Horacio, buoyed up momentarily by the seaworthiness of his craft, or perhaps its riverworthiness.

'Where will she go?' The doctor imagined the paper drawing water in minutes, the suck and pull of her sinking.

'It'll be some sort of holiday – to new places – to see a little more of the world than she has previously seen. Flavia has never left Buenos Aires, and as she joked the other day, it's never too late.'

In the Athenaeum Club fourteen men of irrefutable influence, in dark suits and silk ties that vary in colour but not in sobriety, sit around a teak table that was made four hundred years ago. They look at Gellhorn as if she has just arrived from Mars. But she is aflame with conviction, and having already convinced one roomful of such men, she feels able to browbeat these cynics. Tonight will be a new pitch, and she will not be using notes. These are the publishers, the booksellers, the distributors, the advertising agency guys – not to mention a sprinkling of venture capitalists not known for their philanthropy.

'Gentlemen, thank you for your time. Let me start by reminding you about some of the virtues of our society. We live in a city that has a thousand bookshops – some of them are represented here this evening – and in every community in the land there are shops that try to keep the latest titles in stock. But since the peso was devalued books are expensive commodities – out of the reach of the ordinary man and woman on the street. And not just them. Only a week ago I met a professor at the University of La Plata who teaches comparative literature and she told me she can't compare literatures as much as she would like because the library's budget has been cut, and she certainly can't afford to buy the latest books by Soyinka, Bolaño, Pamuk and so on on her salary.

'We are a nation that has offered a dazzling range of authorial voices to the world, a chorus of voices that proclaims "We are here and our lives are worth recording." But our children can't read these works because the municipal libraries are empty: you can see shelves which have nothing on them other than labels. Go down to any one of them – libraries in Salta, Junín, San Rafael and Puerto Madryn – and you'll find something that resembles a closing down sale. On average there are forty people waiting for each title – yes, each and every title. In my own library there are over two hundred people waiting to read Borges' poetry alone. So this is the answer we've come up with.'

She reaches for fourteen cardboard bound copies of Sabato's first novel, *El Túnel*, and hands them around.

'Each volume will have a recycled binding, and every page will be made of paper that is a hundred per cent recycled. If we manufacture these every child and young person will be able to read, will be able to start their own libraries. And it won't be costly, as every major newspaper publisher in Argentina has said we can print them at their presses when they're lying idle, a couple of hours a day.'

The gathering is incendiary at first – even though what they've heard is slightly better than the vexing version which had been circulating via Chinese whispers and jungle drums before the meeting. They see their own sales dwindling to nothing in a moment. But Phyllida says that this can only create a fresh new appetite among adults and they should remember that all of these young readers will all too soon grow to be adult book buyers, and then she clinches it by saying that monies will be made available to buy the copyrights for the cardboard books and mentions a substantial sum already earmarked by the Banco Nacional.

Some of the arguments Phyllida hears marshalled against her plan are snobbish ones. One book buyer for a major chain suggests that she is degrading the works by wrapping them in discards, but she counters his claims with the withering cliché that he is judging a book by its cover. One man argues that in a country with so many cattle on such huge stretches of pampas they could afford leather-bound copies but she says that this is also about giving street boys a pride in what they do, and, eventually, a way out of their poverty traps. Better than boxing, rock music or drug dealing as passports. And then Victor Sanchez, the owner of the longest chain of bookshops in the country starts clapping, joined quickly by a caucus of his friends. Phyllida knows she has the book trade on her side. Or in the palm of her beautiful hand.

During the course of the next few weeks – and it does only take weeks – the plan blossoms, then fructifies. There are days when big news presses, usually silent for some six hours in the huge industrial estates, work full pelt, sending the first copies to be bound further down the line. Some of the country's leading artists have volunteered to paint original covers for the books; some create bright Rorschach blots and belts of colour, while others create work of more conventional conception.

The most famous and lauded conceptual artist in the land, Oscar Martinelli, though well into his nineties, produces ten covers a day, each and every one of them among his finest works. As a series they gather everything he has ever learned or intuited about life, culminating in a haunting study of a skull, made of glass or crystal and seemingly illuminated from within, with all the fissures of bone turning into gossamer threads. Little canyons of sentience and knowing. Unbeknown to him he has just created the iconic summary of the project, which will become the symbol of the whole endeavour. Nine hundred artists will work on twenty thousand copies of the first print run of Borges' poems, customizing the covers. They reflect their own regions – from the astonishing flatnesses of the pampas to the terrifying and empty vastnesses of Patagonia. A man from Salta, who works in acrylics, depicts the colourful front doors which are so typical of the place, echoing images of the Georgian doors of Dublin, and a man of Welsh descent tells the story of his people coming to Patagonia, with a cover showing a ship, another showing a sheep fence and another a detail from a teacup which tells the whole story – like reading the story of a Grecian urn as you turn it in your hand.

In the series launch, in the Libreria Oriental, the largest bookshop in all of South America, with a million and a half titles on its shelves, the people mingle amid the buzz of a honeycomb covered with worker bees. There are the politicians in their Armani suits, and the press with their weasel snouts, and the glitterati of the Zona Norte where the rich houses reach all the way from Olivos to San Isidro. A huge brass orchestra plays – two hundred members in all – and there is feasting and an auction for the first volume. This appeals to the brazen appetite of the nouveau riche who crave ownership of anything exclusive, and show off their wealth whenever they can: their wives' handbags always come from Prada or Hermes, their life values come from glossy magazines.

For the first book of its kind the auctioneers extract a king's ransom from El Capitan, the owner of the yacht club and marina at Puerto Olivas, who is then happy to present it to the National Library as a gift. His style.

On the wall outside the opulence and extreme comfort of the Libreria a small boy smiles down from a huge poster. He has a copy of a book in his huge hand. Jaime is about to grow into a symbol of the city and, before too long, a symbol of the country itself. Like the starving child of Biafra, or the pathetic child who haunts the adverts for *Les Misérables* in any city worth its salt, it is a young face laden with meaning. But unlike those poster kids for poverty and shame, Jaime's face carries a burden of dignity. Yes, Jaime, who will one day win an enormous literary prize in the States after spending a decade being feted by the world's best universities. The face of a better future for his country . . .

Because there will be cardboard books for every child in Argentina, and cheap writing paper aplenty for every school. One day this boy on the poster will stand before the United Nations, in a specially convened meeting of UNESCO, and he will raise the spectre of illiteracy in order to explain how they banished it from their land, along with the Sony reader and other devices designed to rob one of the simple experience of turning pages and learning.

In May 2023, Jaime addresses a packed chamber and he doesn't have a script, just a narrative of pride:

'Because someone reads with his right hand – depending on which hand one normally uses of course – we know when the end is approaching in, say a Sherlock Holmes story by Conan Doyle, by the number of pages left to turn. Our minds are forced to speed up, to try to solve the crime before the detective. There is a communion between reader and writer, a physical link between them as the hand holds the page, and that link is stronger now the world over, as reading not only threatens to become the new rock and roll but is the new rock and roll. Knowledge is power, as they say and the old ways of disseminating knowledge are often the best ways. So thank you all for supporting the Year of the Book. We will banish illiteracy. We will create people who can think their way out of the world's ills. The answers are all there in some book or other: we just need plenty of detectives to ferret them out. But the future for now, belongs to science fiction, to William Gibson and Phillip K. Dick. But soon it will belong to the unborn millions, waiting to overcrowd the teeming tenements of Buenos Aires and Mumbai, to inhabit the skyscrapers of Singapore and Sydney. To plant their homegrown shacks on every map, to build them in a night, to stake their claims. And they shall have books, I tell you, no matter how poor they are. Because with books you have richnesses beyond comparison.'

The two men are carrying the old lady, who has shrunk to pretty much nothing during the past few months. She weighs no more than fifty loaves, if that. As they turn the corner of the stairs the boy who delivers the piles of papers appears, as if he knows that every effort and sinew in his wiry arms and taut muscles will be called for. Soon, he is working his shoulder under the keel of the boat, taking most of the weight.

A song from the misty recesses of memory echoes in Horacio's skull under his floppy fedora – that song about a grey afternoon and the absence of love. He looks at his wife, whose breathing is shallow now – like a child holding its breath – as she leaves for her final journey. He imagines the accompaniment, coming in unbidden and gently . . .

> How much do I want to cry
> In this grey afternoon?
> The tinkling rain
> Seems to speak about you.
> Forgiveness,
> That it is my fault,
> That I will not see you again
> Never ever, never see you again:
> With my eyes shut
> I see as if it were yesterday
> Shaking, pleading for my love,
> Today your voice comes back to me
> This grey afternoon . . .

The city is preternaturally quiet – grey layers of silence settling to form the bedrock of darkness – with only the very occasional taxi ferrying a drunk to some down-at-heel bordello. The men walk on, coping with the awkward shape of their cargo. Jaime isn't sure what's in the boat, but he can imagine. When they put it down he glimpses a white dress and a lady seemingly asleep.

The men do not speak a word. Horacio listens to the silence, which reflects his inner emptiness. The doctor listens to the reassurance of his own beating heart. Their lungs collectively rasp in the cold night air. They work their way down one street and then another, until they reach the park that runs down to the river. In the distance is the permanent flame near Edificio Kennedy, which commemorates the bloody battles of the Malvinas, but Horacio doesn't see its flickering light, or the lines of the railway tracks beyond or the shape of his friend as he walks behind him. His mind is a swirl of ribbon-like memories that snake and furl into and over each other as he pieces together his married life. The shards of it, now a variegated lapidary of memory.

A confluence of kisses on cherry lips seemingly all summer long – that first splendid summer when he was aflame with young desire and she insisted on guarding her virtue, playing safe and wriggling like an eel when necessary – which was pretty near every time they got this far in their foreplay. He remembers the look on her father's face when they met for the first time – a look of scrutiny and, well, envy, even though he didn't challenge her father's eyes as they flashed with the imagined loss of his only daughter. He recalls the first dance in the Armenian social hall as he demonstrated his ineptitude by sprouting

51

an extra leg: wincing slightly as he remembers her embarrassment at finding herself on her back on the floor as she tripped over his awkward clodhoppers, then blaming her own clumsiness to let him off the hook. These are his memories as the three men walk though the park and the path turns silver in the revealing first light and birds start to twitter exploringly and some of the denizens of the cardboard shanties start to stir. Horacio remembers her laughter, great falling cascades of laughter, the best sound in all the world, and the taste of the skin on her shoulder, which was sweeter than that of the delicious length of her back which had overtones of caramel and notes of honeysuckle, he would swear to God it did, and one day he said he'd now kissed her everywhere, but she said *not quite everywhere* before offering him her deepest secret, and in the dark he found her salty and warm, a cave of brine, a volcano, a heat so fierce it threatened to set his hair on fire.

These are Horacio's memories of his wife, gathered as a tangerine line of light on the horizon thickened, as the sun sets another Argentine day ablaze. He remembers that too, filtered from all the other memories for whatever reason some things stick and others turn to mist.

The men are on the riverbank now – next to the crazy golf course. The doctor suggests they should now conduct some small ritual, for it is almost time.

'A ritual?'

'Yes, even we humanists should mark the occasion. It's the end of a long journey, Horacio . . .'

It is the first time he's used the man's first name, that

he's dispensed with the doctor-patient courtesies. It sounds clumsy to the two of them. The boy wanders off to look at one of the constructions on the golf course – a windmill and a dyke, invoking the Netherlands.

River light corruscates. The surf of traffic grows louder on the overpasses. Colour leeches into the sepia. Day begins its struggles and satisfactions. This is Flavia's day and the one her husband dreads.

'It's a special day . . .'

Before the doctor can finish his sentence Horacio starts to sing – one of the very old songs, one of the primitive songs that can tear the heart's cage apart, and the young lad starts to sing as well, in notes struck from pure gold and then the doctor adds a baritone as velvety as Guinness as they raise the boat and settle it unfussily on the water. For a few moments the boat does nothing but then Horacio prompts it to move by prodding it with a stick and his wife leaves them now, taking with her the news of her long year's battle with illness. She begins to move with the current and the ship looks like a swan, the white of her nightgown like a soft duvet of feathers and then the song changes as the old man's tears flow and he starts to bay like a terrier that's stepped on a nail.

The current takes her away more steadily now and Horacio utters guttural sounds, cronks like a raven or a crow and the doctor takes the young man's hand as they watch the small craft pick up some speed, say two knots and rising, and even though it is made of paper it doesn't sink but rather it looks surprisingly steady and solid, breasting the wavelets as if it is a rubber inflatable. It starts to move to mid-channel where trees are carried down from way upriver where uprooted stumps from the leftover forests are a danger to shipping – any ship, that is, and most certainly one made up of old copies of *La Nación* and *Ambito Financiero*. After a half hour which feels like an Ice Age, Horacio has settled a little and his sobs are rhythmic now. They stand there on a crumbling breakwater as three eyewitnesses watch the señora moving out of hailing reach, out to open water, to open sea, eventually. Horacio's gaze is unwaveringly steady. May a fair wind follow you, dear. My great love. Farewell.

Later that day Horacio feels with his fingertips the shape of his wife in the lumpy mattress, ferreting for the last physical memory of her. Horacio drinks deeply from the glass of aguardiente next to the bed. He won't get up again until he himself is summoned by death. Until it is time to see her again. The doctor knocks on the door, for maybe the third time that day, and then goes away again. The old man, stubborn and inebriate, hugs the coverlet.

But in the morning, in a fog of sorrow cloaking a lagoon of worry, he feels as if a psychotic blacksmith has been reshaping his skull with a bull hammer, flattening his occipitus. He remembers his wife's words about attempting to speak to him from the world beyond, and leaves his bed to look for the letter confirming the appointment she'd had. The Head of Department was called Professor Sophocles, no less. Horacio rang him from the phone in the street and asked if his wife had made contact yet.

'Nothing's come through, so far, Señor Trucco, but we'll let you know just as soon as we hear anything. I can guarantee that . . .'

He makes it sound as if they were regularly linked up with the afterworld. Had their conduits in place.

And from that moment on Horacio was alert to her presence, taking a pencil and paper with him everywhere and waiting for an invisible hand to guide his own and spell out the code. He even bought a child's abacus, thinking that might make things simpler. But 4557759990003428190 never came through, for all the intensity of his vigil.

The next morning it had been arranged that Manuelito should take Jaime out for breakfast – one more attempt, and perhaps the last, to build a bridge them, between two continents seemingly drifting apart. The cook in the Mexican restaurant had an enormous girth that matched his reputation and you would have backed him over all comers in a tortilla-eating competition. He had a great reputation for making *huevos rancheros,* the best in the known universe. Jaime had stared through the windows of the place more than once, amazed at the number of people who were willing to queue for food there, a serpentine line that sometimes stretched right round the block. But these were no ordinary recipes. They were handed down as family heirlooms from the cook's grandmother, Claudia Benitez, who had placed them in an envelope under seal in a bank deposit box, to wait there until the chef was old enough to appreciate them. He did just that, treasuring the sepia pieces of paper, aware of how small words, a hint of Turkish mint, a zip of lime, could become an ambrosial taste.

'I hear you've got yourself a splendid new job, or should I call it a role in life? I've seen the posters and you look quite wonderful.'

Perhaps it was something to do with the quality of the eggs – which came from rare varieties – Houdans and Norfolk Greys – or maybe the calibre of the chorizo or the butter from Junín but Jaime started to tell him everything, about Señora Gellhorn who had seen him on the street one night and how she had just arranged for him to be the model for a series of new book covers following on from the success of the posters for which he had originally modelled – and how strange was that word on the boy's lips – and how she had also given his uncle a full-time job so he had sold the shop. As Jaime told Manuelito about all this the boy reached into his bag and, his face welling up with pride, he showed Manuelito the very first prototype book, which the señora had used to persuade the President himself to back her plan. There he was, on the cover, beaming. He handed the book to his friend, only realizing as he passed it above the salt and pepper pots that he saw him as a friend. Fazed, Manuelito started to read. He is properly embarrassed.

'No, not from the beginning,' said Jaime. 'Pick a bit from the middle. I haven't got there yet.'

'"And a shadow of death fell across the young girl's face. You can expect to lose a father or mother and even, sometimes, the two, but losing a brother is a rupture in the very order of things, like Lady Macbeth tearing out a baby from her womb before its time."'

'It isn't exactly a happy story,' said Jaime, his mouth full of eggs.

'Not at all – but there are only seven kinds of story and one of them has to be the sad sort.'

'Seven?' asked Jaime. 'What are the others?'

And as Manuelito started to list them and explain them – the various orders of narrative he'd learned by heart at evening classes – and talked in detail about how books had dealt with dark times in history and how poetry had failed to deal with the chicos who went to the Malvinas but left the Falklands and men who went as heroes came back as losers who would never be mentioned in a song, Jaime looked at him as if for the first time. On the jukebox in the restaurant, a tune he knew was playing, one he'd heard seeping under the old couple's door. He would miss the sound of their soft shuffle behind the closed door. A soft piano lilt, a cracked voice joining the one in the recording.

> *Llega el viento del recuerdo aquel*
> *Al rincon de mi abandono*
> *Y entre el polvo muerto del ayer*
> *Tambien volver tu querer*
> *Yo no ne si viviras feliz*
> *O si el mundo ha vencido*
> *Si viviendo sin querer vivir*
> *Buscas la paz de morir*

> A memory like a breeze comes to meet me
> In a corner of abandonment

And in yesterday's great dust
Your love has returned
I don't know if you'll live happily
Or if the world will defeat you
If you will live without wanting life
If you want peace by leaving the earth.

Out at sea the small boat rose and fell with the wave curls as they became bigger now that the the hurricane season had opened with some peremptory gusts. The undertow was the sound of a double bass, sonorous and deeply fluid, the whiteness of the notes lifting up like a saint's hands explaining a miracle. And high above, a single albatross, on a long sojourn from New Zealand, was leading the way.

Chapter 2

All at Sea

The men are barely home before the weather turns, out in the estuary, as a buckshot of rain spits down from heavy slate-coloured clouds which come in from nowhere. It is jet-propelled by a drunken wind that drives water onto land in one ferocious, cold breath. The returning mourners buckle under the ferocity of the pelting water. But it's not the half of what she'll have to face on her journey.

Flavia's delicate craft will have to withstand winds from all directions and of all magnitudes. Coming at her from all points. NNW, N, NE and at one stage the scientifically impossible EW. She'll encounter the Barber, be marooned by the Simoom, face the gusts of the Cape Doctor and Blue Norther, the Pali, the Mauka and the indescribable Knik. The Sirocco will blow heat hazily at her, as will the Santa Ana, off to take its oxygen to stoke up bushfires in the Sierras. There'll be the Cordonazo and the Papagayos in their turn, but none will harm her.

Wafted by gentler breezes such as the Sundowner and Cockeyed Bob, the craft will float sedately, like a single water lily adrift on the tide. But usually the winds will be more severe, more testing, kicking up a storm – churn wind and hurl wind and whip wind, hell wind keening and turning the waves to a wild broth, storm gales to toss her, typhoons to wreck her, all the danger winds from all the

59

compass points, agitations of wind, devastations of energy, all able to turn the paper craft into mulch in a moment. But they do not. One of the transatlantic gales will be strong enough to pick up a Shaker chair from a backyard in Maine and carry it across a whole wide expanse of ocean, to deposit it, gently and unbroken, in a lighthouse garden at Nash Point in Wales. The cushion on its seat still in place.

There are winds of great variety. Fog winds conceal winds of madness, chill blow melds with rain breeze, all manner of gust and breath, but as yet no apocalypse wind, the one that blows once and for ever, snuffing out time itself. There'll be waves the height of the Eiffel Tower and higher, much higher – the height of the Sears Tower – wet, green cathedrals bowing into themselves, giant domes of surge and effect, a Chartreuse flow heading straight for her, all wild bells in the rigging and numberless tons of water wanting nothing more than to fall down on the small craft and obliterate her.

Were she in a big ship such as the *Ark Royal,* it would be dangerous enough. In her cradle of paper it's unbelievable that she hasn't gone under. The little craft is hurled from side to side, over one sudden steep wall of wave to be smashed against another, before shifting on to a video game. A video game? From the right vantage point that's what it looks like.

Two hundred miles away and three hours earlier there had been a massive storm upriver. Trees were felled by the deluge as their roots were made bare, and these were huge trees which had stood for years, for centuries some of them, but one and all their heavy trunks and flailing

60

branches were scooped along by the waves. Any one of them could have pulverized the boat, turned it into papier mâché.

The albatross, which was following the boat's course as would a mascot, a flying familiar, would have noticed that it seemed to be moved by some force that allowed it to avoid collision, as if some deity had an Xbox joystick in its grip, that this was the brand new Rivercraze game on PlayStation. Huge tree at nine o' clock! Over she goes, safe to mid-channel, away and away from the river rage. Three hundred points and a new life. Two trunks heading straight for her! A slight flick to the left and she's avoided them with ease, milliseconds to spare. Six hundred points. A tree so huge it's still got chattering monkeys huddling in its leaves. Use a spare life and leap the next level, leaving the terrified gibbons well behind. Bonus. Ping! Ping! Today's highest score. Congratulations!

And in a series of miraculous moves Flavia's little craft leaves the enormous estuary and goes out to the sea proper and its dangers. A huge ship, the Cape of Good Light, carrying 30,000 enormous metal boxes heads straight for her and comes within nautical yards of smashing her, but still it seems as if the River God is looking out for her and has handed on responsibility to the Sea God, who is similarly benign.

Over the weeks, Flavia's boat explores the invisible labyrinths of currents, egged on by wind, through days of storm and calm alike, and some days when the millpond sea is a lake of mercury. She cleaves through that water of unutterable stillness, leaving a single silver trail in her wake although Flavia, the astonishing traveller, doesn't move a jot, not so much as twitch a nerve.

Sometimes the horizon is rent in two by a scream which seems to come from great depth, the thunder of the world, which is Horacio emptying out his grief, so that the terrible sound carries without echo across limitless oceans.

The old man can't breathe for the pain of her absence, as if he is trapped in an Iron Maiden, his lungs like a flattened accordion. She is on a voyage without him, and they always went places together. They should sail together. If he could will it to be thus it would happen. She is a sail in a boat he has glued together with love, believing that hope would charge her sails like the wind.

It is a paper boat and yet a magnet. Migrating birds land on her and one tiny bird, a red-eyed vireo, weakened awfully by the buffeting of wind, settles on Flavia's closed eyelids. She is a statue, unheeding of the feathery fluttering. And following the boat is the albatross, present every day, able to sleep on the wing if need be.

The bird had been though quite a picaresque episode in its life leading up to moment it spotted the small craft, feeling compelled to follow it, much as whales seek busy flocks of seabirds to alert them to food under the waves. Before long even the albatross would have to turn for home but not yet, not quite yet.

It was born on Campbell Island, a stupendous rock near the southernmost tip of New Zealand's South Island. Because it was a young bird it had a strong desire to wander. It didn't need to find a mate as yet, so it loved to veer with the wind and shear the waves.

It saw the South Pole as it flew over endless acres of ice, and got caught up in the mighty winds that funnelled around the Horn. Here it caught sight of serried ranks of penguins dressed as if in tuxedos, standing among the spindrift and weed. It was attacked by a skua, that most piratical of birds, but it outmanoeuvred the bird with its deadly, hatchet bill, putting on a display of acrobatics that would have delighted a human observer. It was a testing trial for the young bird. The whole aerial trek was a long, arduous, testing rite of passage over many, many leagues. By the time he returned he would be worthy of a mate.

When the albatross reached the coasts of South America it was tired and disorientated. It was found by two biologists, its limp body spent of all energy, on a remote beach in Patagonia. Still, after two weeks of eating dog food mixed with water, and the agreeable company of the dog itself – a black labrador named Mascot which had a long, wet tongue – the bird felt sufficiently strong and determined to venture onwards. It would be another two years before it found its way to Otago Head, and a further two before it looked into the famished craw of its first chick.

The boat moved swiftly now, following the race of the wind and the pulse of the current. When the wind abated a little, and calm descended upon the sea's surface, curious sea mammals pushed their snouts over the sides, threatening to capsize it with their submarine weight. Whales, too, followed as if magnetized by the craft, which exerted a pull similar to that which takes them along their ancient routes in the sea, from Alaska to the Sea of Cortez and then back again.

Flavia's boat went through the Sargasso Sea and crossed the Bermuda Triangle (and came out safely from one side of it, unlike so many craft, such as the *Marionetta*, the *Giant Sook*, USS *Cyclops* and the SS *Marine Sulphur Queen* along with an astonishing number of aircraft, including three US fighter aircraft, the infamous 'Lost Squadron'). Above an underwater trench, deeper than the imagination, somewhere beyond the near horizon, the boat attracted the attention of one of the monsters of the deep, a leviathan half a mile long, which surfaced for the first time in twenty years. It craned towards the surface on a long neck like a brontosaurus. It possessed a mouth like a gigantic sea-cave, with teeth like monumental sailor's headstones. Two blind eyes above tunnel-like nostrils. And when the gargantuan head surfaced it was like a huge periscope. This was a Pleistocene remnant, sent for by Flavia.

The sonar and radar paraphernalia on board the *Nisshin Maru* went haywire. This was the flagship of the Japanese whaling fleet and they had never encountered anything like this. It had been a long journey and the crew was jaded, tired of playing cat-and-mouse on the high seas with the ships from Greenpeace and Sea Shepherd, which had tried to stymie them and the rest of the flotilla at every nautical turn. The Captain would have been happy, and deliriously so, to steer his craft straight for them, willing to destroy these interlopers who understood nothing about the relationship between his people and the sea. Such impudence. Such unashamed meddling. He would behead every last one of them. American scum. Let heads roll from shoulders.

In the north of North America native peoples were given the right to hunt whales and yet these other soft Americans saw nothing ironic about playing hide-and-seek in order to stop the Japanese hunting. It was all too hypocritical. What with the whale populations on the rise and all.

Not that this trip had too much evidence of that. There hadn't been a blip on the sonar for days. They planned to head down to the reserve, catch themselves some southern whales. Nip in and nip out once they'd shaken off the lily-livered liberals. But then the dials went wild. Something like the shape of an enormous butterfly cocoon . . .

'There's something enormous in the water! One of the biggest white whales I've ever seen in all my days,' shouted Lieutenant Kawabata, misidentifying the shape through no fault of his own. He ascribed the scale of the pulsing white blob on the screen to his own fatigue, as he'd been kept awake by Dexedrine from the sick bay these past three weeks. They were understaffed on the bridge so the hours were punishing. The men on the bridge looked like automata working the controls.

'Let's claim this scalp,' said the captain. 'Load the harpoons. All crew on standby.'

'Right away, Captain,' said Kawabata, hallucinating like billy-o, his lips feeling rubbery. A samurai warrior's hand crawled out of his coffee mug and flexed its fingers and all the rings on them. A yellow-and-black asp curled itself around his coffee spoon.

Rainbow Warrior III might have been able to help them. Maybe. By the time the crew of the *Nisshin Maru* had realized their mistake it was too late. They were following a creature the size of a city block in Tokyo and although they didn't know it, they were just following the calf – the mother was still surfacing from the furthermost recesses of the trench. When she arrived, following her offspring to the surface through black water to glass-bottle-green layers and finally breaching through shards of turquoise, cerulean and ultramarine, her tail flipped over and completely destroyed the factory ship, sending broken pieces of crew member mixed freely with mangled messes of hull down to Davy Jones's locker. The ship was well-nigh obliterated, as thoroughly as if connected packages of plastic explosives had detonated in the heart of her.

One moment, the flagship of the fleet, pearl of the oceans was steaming ahead and the next she was scuppered, sunk with little trace.

By the time the *Warrior* got to them – attracted by their Mayday signals – it was evident that no one had survived the catastrophe. It had been destroyed by a mighty force, as evidenced by the wide arc of debris. The biologists on board swore blue they'd picked up something enormous on their sonar but it proved too big for their calibrations. Too big, mind!

'It was like something out of Spielberg,' said Morgensen, flapping with excitement.

'Bigger than anything else in the known world,' nodded his colleague Anthurst.

But the creature had gone beyond technology and its

66

tracking. It had plummeted to the bottom of the abyss, where not a photon of light could reach it.

No one saw the little boat a quarter of a mile away, away from the massacre and the mess, as the mythical animal sank down into water that was Bible-black, away from all light, with its calf the size of a football stadium swimming placidly alongside her gently undulating tail. They had emerged from the trench to protect a woman. What instinct drove them, goodness only knows.

Flavia could have made landfall at almost any port, or just drifted onto a storm beach, moving as she was with the wind and thus almost as fast as the wind. La Guaira, for instance, the entrance to Caracas, a city infected by craziness, where the rule of law had been replaced by the Lord of Misrule. One murder every twenty minutes in a city that had abandoned faith as being too forlorn, or too bloodily compromised by the moral despotism of the place. No faith other than voodoo, which now worshipped the dead gangsters who once controlled the barrios, the streets and sprawling shanties, placing live cigarettes in the mouths of china models of these hoodlums. Here they worship violence. That's how bad it is. They're crackers in Caracas.

Or what about Dar es Salaam? East Africa. A paradisiacal place at first glance. A lapis lazuli stretch of water where dhows with startling white sails ply to and fro between the mainland and Zanzibar, carrying perfumes and spices, coconuts and dried fish. Frankincense from Oman via Aden. Cloves and cinnamon sufficient to make the boats smell like souks. But you can't dine off the scenery, and there is stultifying poverty that can turn men into wretches, even as the sun rising like a silver bauble above the early morning mangroves makes the place seem worth the world. Yet here too there are murders galore, and they are mainly of albinos, or rather albinistic children: these are the spirits, or Zeru-Zeru, killed to order for witch-doctor rituals.

One night a woman called Salma was given orders by these clandestine men to dress her white-haired and white-skinned daughter in black from head to foot and then put her to sleep in a cabin by herself. Salma knew that she had to obey the orders of the tribal elders. She had no choice. Some hours later, a gang of men carrying machetes entered the cabin and cut off the girl's legs, then proceeded to drink her blood.

In Dar es Salaam an albino hand is worth two million shillings, or a thousand pounds sterling. A man was once caught carrying a baby's head en route for the Congo where a doctor had promised to pay for it by the ounce. It looked up at the customs men from a little sack, the eyes milky.

Beyond the startlewhite of the dhows, in turquoise waters where sharks swim in needle-toothed squadrons, a small paper boat is scything through the choppy waves. Moving as if through a dream.

On she goes, the little spirit craft. Through all the wonders of the seven seas. On she goes.

Chapter 3

Welcome to Oakland

37° 48′ N 122 °16′ E

If a city builds itself on reputation just as much as asphalt and concrete then this is a city that will withstand the coming earthquakes of history. It's a city of prizefighter grit, with an aptitude for both controlled and sudden violence. Riots flare up almost casually to set city streets alight, cars lighting up like gasoline beacons. Slayings and murders are the staples of the evening news. Gangs run rampant in some parts of town. But that's to forget all the good stuff, the quiet piano lessons, the browsed books in Pegasus, the familial laughter, the watering of exuberant house plants by old ladies on La Salle who remember this town when it was jumping, and life was awash with scrupulously mixed martinis. Their husbands' memories are well tended, up at the Chapel of the Chimes, one of life's beautiful buildings. When they go to join them they'll have words like *It was a good life* on their dessicated and chapped lips. Final utterances. *I'm coming to see you.*

Look at the scaup and other ducks diving for mussels in Lake Merritt when the January air is Tibetan in its clarity, or the Chinese folk in immaculate silks syncopate their t'ai chi under the elms, or the way the houses on the Oakland hills look like Dalmatia, or the silvery snake of the channel over towards San Leandro glints instantly as the fog rolls away, a grey quilt replaced by bright tapestry. Turkey buzzards execute lazy figures of eight over the freeways. Eucalyptus branches snap in the heat. Tell me then that this is just a gritty city.

There is a sound that sums up the place, from the throats of men, the hawkers who sell the *Tribune*, uttering cries that sounded like any words other than *Tribune,* standing on their traditional spots whatever the weather. *Gremitode! Marsone!* Guttural. Feral. Language cut loose. But they're a dying breed, these sellers. People don't get newsprint on their fingers anymore.

And the city's other sounds. Rap thumping as if it has emerged from the earth's mantle, the bass bins a geological rumble. The foghorns of Alameda, drifting in to the almighty port. The constant air traffic of Southwest Airlines, banking over the length of the San Mateo Bridge as they come in from Burbank and leave for Portland, spreading their liveried wings over the gleaming salt pans, crystalline white in the bleaching sunlight. And the tribal yelling of Raiders' fans at the Coliseum, like a convention of cavemen who've just learned how to open beer cans. Or baseball fans, inspired by statistics, watching the players' stately progression, and the radio commentators, tinnily relayed into personal headphones, speaking the poetry of sliders in the dirt. The high pitch of displaced air as BART cars cruise along lengths of tunnel. It's unlike the sight and sound of any other subway. London is slower, a cranking Victorian mass transit, with everyone smelling everyone else's intimate scents and handing on chest colds like free gifts. The Tokyo Metro is as efficient as keyhole surgery. Paris smells of chicory and stale Gitanes cigarettes. But the Bay Area is two-tone, both a keening and a whoosh as the ten-car train for Pittsburgh Bay Point or Pleasanton arrives on its electric rail.

It's a dozen local radio stations, disseminating anything from cool jazz to frantic mariachi, from music to which lounge lizards can mate to classical expression, Bruckner or Mahler beamed in live from Vienna or Toronto. It's the surf of the freeways meeting in spaghetti loops over lots in Emeryville. The sound of Brazilian pop and freshets of laughter coming from the new cocktail bars that spring open downtown. But more than anything else it's that hip hop. The sound of the street, urgent, urban, coming to get you.

Tierra Doon's innocence was shattered in a second when her brother was shot last year. Before that she'd been a typical kid, part of the Disney family, mad on Pixar, while Barney, the dumb-ass bear on TV, was probably her best friend. Probably. She'd spot Bambi nibbling grass shoots in the park near the basketball hoops. Big Bird sometimes waddled by the Black and White Liquor Store. Captain Nemo dived through her dreams. In the world of her young and fecund imagination she lived in quite the selfsame world as Little Princess. There were times when she could transform the dump where she lived into a palace, such that her room would glow in golden light and bluebirds circled the turrets through a honey light that wasn't from the streetlights drifting in through tears in the curtains.

71

The palace was built of silver bricks and the turrets had red roofs under a star-spangled sky, which was dissected by rainbows arcing through, even if it was night. Here, in the castle grounds, grown-ups smiled all the time and there was always something nice to eat. Public ice cream faucets around the moat. But all that was shattered with a single gunshot. Her world was rent in two. The time before and the time after. Afterwards Tierra believed in Satan and hatred, all because of the naked hurt that tore at her insides.

She didn't want to see the place where he'd died, down in that part of the city where the streets have no names, only numbers. It's the part of Oakland that can't afford street names, way beyond the Coliseum. The reason they build the mega stadia in such run-down parts is the low cost of land. The Superdome in New Orleans. The ragged army of homeless folk sleeping near the Padres' new home in San Diego. No-gos. Dead real estate. But Tierra had to accompany her mother, to keep her company. As they approached the sheeted ground, with what seemed like the shape of a sleeping, supine figure under the yellow tarpaulin, her fingers squeezed those of her mother so hard she thought she could hear the calcium of her bones crumbling.

Under the tarp lay her brother Antony. Ten yards away, under another untidy blanket, lay his friend Monte Parkes. There was no blood or anything like that to suggest that Ant was lying there, or why he was lying there. But her mother's face did, twisted in a contorted grotesquerie of pain. His absence pierced her. She had new lines on her forehead already as another violent, needless death etched itself into the face of an Oakland mother.

They called him Nu Nu at home, because when she was small Tierra couldn't say Antony so she made the nearest sound to it, pursing her small lips with concentration. But Nu Nu was dead, killed at random by a man whose brains were fried and frazzled, all cranked up by crystal meth.

Another meaningless death in the big city. Life is like an HBO series, watched on one of the outsize plasma screens that loom over even the poorest living rooms in America. The idiot's lantern, lighting up the faces of the brain dead. And like all good drama series, this city has a killer soundtrack. It's there on every street, on every corner, pounding and pulsing, an aural aorta. It pours out of apartment blocks, from sound systems in all-night diners, shoe shops, food markets. Go buy gas and the guy behind the counter proves that when they say they're open 24/7 they mean it. He gives the impression he's here 24/7 – he has bags under his eyes that look as if they could sleep six – and he is listening to the city's soundtrack. Lil Wayne. Jay-Z. The Coup, big in this town.

Looking for the rhythm, ti-ti-ti-ti-ti-ti-ti. Bam-bam-ba-bam-bam-bam. The sound of the bass, resonant, the undertow of all the tunes, deep as the pull of the ocean. It lies under songs about guns – Walter PPKs, ArmaLites, heavy Magnums. Songs about men who hate. Songs about sex, about the brothers in the hood, and the people of the projects, marooned there. Here life is cheap and life is tough and only the dying is easy. Parts of the city ruled by

Latinos. Others by bros. Divided like a city sacked but without the spoils. Too poor for spoils. Too dirt poor for pretty much anything if you get on the wrong side of the tracks, now that the trains don't run and the tracks are silent. But it'll be the niggas who take the streets, finally. Strength in numbers, brothers in arms. That's what the song says. That's what the motherfucking song heralds. A new age.

A flash of electric blue above the substation. The tang of ozone like an Amtrak train hauling itself to a stop. Bodies on the street. Blood on the sidewalk. The machine mirrors some drum rimshots. Ti-ti-ti-ti-ti-ti-tisk-tisk. And the level of the bass rises now, the volume increases as if the speakers will have to blow, platetectonic rumble with enough subsonic reverberation to bring the 'scrapers down and all the other buildings in the town. Shaking the Ethiopian hair salons and the taco stands, the car salesrooms along Broadway with their automobile litany – Lexus, Honda, Chevrolet, Toyota – and all the little businesses that sell Szechuan food, hard liquor, dry beans, hot flesh, two-for-one deals, all the tiendas and midnight stores, the mall outlets and specialist supplies. Along International Boulevard and Clay and Lakeshore and College – they are all shaking gently, away from the epicentre of the big bass bins. Tisk-tisk-tisk-tisk-tisk. Ba-bam-bam-bam. The hip hop is ever present.

And there's a simple refrain. Motherfucka, motherfucka, see me now motherfucka – and above all this, competing with the searing words, there's a guitar break – like one of Prince's most inspired riffs. But it's not Prince singing, oh

74

no. This no-name rapper certainly seems upset about things, is a lot more ferocious about the way he confronts the world, facing up to it, facing it down. This is a man giving voice to the deprived suburbs – a Compton voice, like NWA. Or a Tupac, giving it up for East Harlem. While Prince, the fey pixie king of Minnesota, has a voice in angelic registers, the rappers of this town, of this hood, make the gravelly sounds of hot tarmac, mixed with acrid nicotine smoke and sewer mist escaping from manhole covers. In this song the singer sounds as if he got out of bed on the wrong side, if he ever made it to bed. With blood on his hands and steel in his heart.

Every city has its rappers, rhyming in dialect, keeping it real. From the interminable decay of Detroit to the palm trees and watery glare of Miami hip hop is as ubiquitous as Coca Cola. Here, in this proud, loud city, Oakland, the band of the hour is The Coup, sending letters out from its broken hood, just as surely as did the Goats from Washington DC and Public Enemy from New York.

Yes, hip hop is everywhere, rattling the darkened windows of the sleek BMWs as they purr away along Fourth, en route for sinister rendezvous in a gap in the security camera cover in the Target parking lot. To sell crank, in commodious quantities, no doubt.

Yes, hip hop. The only battle America's won in some while. But with this one it's complete takeover. Hearts and minds. Attitude and dress sense. Now, this is the world music. Bam-bam-bam. Period.

And it pounds through Oakland days and nights. This city of six hundred thousands citizens with the lake in the middle – the first nature reserve in the United States. Lake Merritt, with its squadrons of pelicans and a bewilderment of buffleheads, so numerous are they, bobbing like corks on the chill water.

Down near the marina you can visit Jack London Square – and you can see the actual cabin where he penned *The Call of the Wild*, even though it has to be admitted that there's another cabin just like it in Vancouver, so it's probably a clone in roughly-hewn logs. And this is one of the cornerstones of city tourism. Desperate. Little wonder then that Gertrude Stein's acerbic words 'There's no there there' plays on their minds – rankling the urban planners, the regenerators, the men with a view if not a vision.

Do you want a souvenir of this town? What about Black Panther Hot Pepper Sauce? The Panthers were founded here, raising fists against oppression. There's a thing. That's a sauce.

Oakland has got one hell of a port, taking in half of China's entire exports to the US and a quarter of all the stuff coming in from Japan, from Ichiban beer to jasmine rice. And people love this city without an obvious heart, adore its grittiness, its lack of pretension, even if a hundred people are murdered here each year. Dangerous streets, indeed. And plenty of ways to die, too – drive-by, mercy-slaying, straight suicide, jealousy bullets, drug-related shoot-outs, accidental ricochet, paid hit, gang blast, mistaken identity, for a few dollars more. Spoiled for choice about ways to be be blasted out of this life.

Mind you, things could be worse. This could be Detroit, where the mortuary vans go out on routine patrol: little wonder music there is shot through with violence and grief. Oakland is like Coney Beach compared with, say Detroit's 8 Mile. And these things matter when it comes to civic pride in today's America. *Well at least we have fewer homicides than Flint or Richmond this year*, say the city elders, wherever they may be. Which means we can cut down on police numbers. Plant some flowers maybe, or repair a road.

The age of the old style Oakland gangs is long gone, other than one remnant, one ageing renegade crew which at this moment is killing time in a lock-up at the back of Bev-Mo. Let's go meet them. And there's one thing patently noteworthy and more than slightly ridiculous about them: they've been watching *Reservoir Dogs* too long. They've combed over every line of this perfect heist movie more times than they have sense, twice a week sometimes, sometimes more during the past three years. It's deep in their DNA by now and they're well on the way to transmuting into Tarantino's lot. Mr White. Mr Pink and so on.

They wear the same clothes as their idols: the sharp, if outmoded suits, the ties, the crisp-collared white shirts, all in all, well heeled. They dress like this in a knowing way, their apparel laced with irony but then they cross the line between fantasy and reality without knowing it. Things get blurred. They quote the film ad nauseam, the lines of dialogue becoming ragged and thin, wind-ripped spider gossamer. Mark Clooney's reached the stage where he *is* rather than *thinks* he is Mr Black while Steve DiMaggio believes he's Mr Pink, not that he looks anything like the spook-eyed Steve Buscemi who plays him in the film – and the same is true for other members of the gang. Metamorphosed. Left their identities behind near a ripped insect husk. So it must be the case that Specky Kravitz is Mr White because he makes the decisions. He has to. Mr Pink can't decide how to get out of bed in the morning, and the others aren't exactly sharp.

Mr White knows the city is changing around them at a pace they cannot comprehend, let alone properly respond to. The competition has them licked, outsmarted, out-manoeuvred, outgunned. The drugs have changed. Specky remembers a time when all the main drugs were white, but then, after Vietnam, heroin came in all brown and then came the multicoloured ecstasy pills, which made the drugs seem childish, not substances to respect. Not men's drugs. Which are white. Clinical white. And as a former junkie Mr White should know about the colour scheme, remembering how the opiate tries to wrestle you to the ground, sap your strength, take away the larger part of you.

Nowadays the Triads run the gambling, the Wu-Tans run prostitution, Latino gangs such as the White Hands are supremely well-organised and are in bed with the unions, who receive a monthly stipend in used notes. This is how criminals find the first rung on legitimacy's ladder. And in a place where cop recruitment is like asking people to swim with vipers, with so many deaths on the job, and the life expectancy not much more than an Atom bomb guinea pig, you can't blame people for not forming an orderly line to join the Police Department. Not when you're strapped to that bomb each time you go out on patrol.

There are places in the city the cops won't go, fearing the hail of automatic gunfire as trigger-happy crankheads open up. The city council's on the take, like everywhere else, so you can build whatever you damn well like as long as the right palms have been crossed with silver, as long as the cash is lodged in the Cayman islands, untraceable as morning mist. It's a rabidly busy wasp's nest of a city: sting or be stung.

And before we take leave of our discourse about the city's ills and strains we should remember it's a city across the water from San Francisco, a city everyone's heard of. Where the tourists binge on clam chowder and crabs' legs at Fisherman's Wharf and max the plastic around Union Square. Where the cable-car wires hum of history and some of the streets are steep enough to test a mountain sherpa's calf muscles. Remember the adrenaline punch of the opening sequence of the *The Streets of San Francisco* where the cars hurtled out into thin air before crashing down on their shock absorbers. Look, there's Chinatown and the Ferry Building. Dine at the Tadich Grill or sip top-shelf cocktails at the Redwood Room. One of the hippest drinking venues on the West Coast. Truly. Make mine an Absolut, neat.

So Oakland is always relegated to position as a second city, playing Melbourne to San Francisco's Sydney, São Paolo to Rio, always second place.

But not when it comes to goods inward: there is that gargantuan port we saw bringing in Asian comestibles and consumables, imported products from three dozen countries. And there is that pride about building a place from hard graft, a no nonsense, knuckles down, tails up sort of place.

And financial indices depend on all those goods coming in and going out.

In London, they collate an index called the Baltic Dry. Each and every day, index canvassers contact companies around the world, asking the cost of ferrying this and that to this port, to that one. What would it cost to take one hundred thousand tonnes of metal from Perth to Hong Kong, or a grain silo's worth of rice from Thailand to Tokyo? From Oakland to Shanghai? There's a song in there somewhere.

The canvassers count all sorts of ships, from the titanic Supramax through the Panamax to the Capesize. It's inevitable that all of them will pass through here eventually. Pass through Suez en route for Oakland. Take evasive action to avoid desperate pirates in the South China Seas, Northern California bound. There are invisible freeways in the sea leading to the docks and derricks and outsize cranes. Bringing poisons, cars, designer labels, illicit drugs, German chemicals, salt pork, fireworks, dried foods, hidden prostitutes, Scotch whisky, fake Scotch whisky. The modern harvest. Bringing in the sheaves. And the noodles.

Saturday morning, Berkeley, just down the freeway from Oakland. Outside the windows of the duplex, the campus campanology society is giving its weekly recital, as they have done these past forty years. An elegant Italianate campanile stands seemingly dead centre of the campus, leading the eye to the mini-pyramid on top. So, at twelve sharp, you will hear bells in pleasing concert.

Half-listening to them, above the hum of air conditioning in the duplex, are David and Elsbetha Kearny, who want to start a family. This morning if they can. Any morning if they can. They've decided not to have sex in the evening as David's so preconditioned to having a glass or two of wine after work, such is the unbridled stress of what he does, that Elsbetha thinks it won't work then: she's been reading too much about booze and fertility and is a tad paranoid about it all. She has amassed a small library of books on the subject of pregnancy and fruitfulness. It is an obsession by now, and a baby is her grail, the supreme trophy at the end of life's contorted path. As contorted as her Fallopians.

There are some who make love to the velvet strains of Barry White, something really-get-down-with-it such as 'You're the First, the Last, my Everything' or 'Can't Get Enough of Your Love, Babe' or something sexy out of Brazil, by Gilberto Gil, maybe, remixed with dub reverb. But on Saturday mornings, when David and Elsbetha get it on – in their world of shame and recrimination, of vitamin supplements and cigarette bans – they do so to the accompaniment of bells, playing a range of music, Ravel and Varèse, strident Stockhausen, and this morning a bright and airy new composition, in the minimal manner, by John Adams. He's a local boy and his latest composition, which uses all the small bells, making the sound of a fairy procession, is passing through the air, banking on shimmery wings as it turns towards the marina. It's a Nepalese sound, a celebration of tiny things, flitting fireflies dancing a roundel in the shrubbery, sending out semaphores of phosphorescence, or antic leprechaun dancers doing a jig around a toadstool. Which makes David and Elsbetha's ridiculous butting of haunches seem more than a little pantomimic, especially when the Varèse starts, all weird time signatures and angular rhythms. The bell ringers sweat in their tower as they stretch out to pull all the ropes. As David works up his own lather.

'Perhaps this time?'

This is his mock-optimistic and tired question. David is beginning to worry about the near permanent ache in his back from the all the humping and bumping. He's pushing fifty-five and imagines himself ending up sicklebacked from the strain, a psychotherapist so physically bent over that all the world will end up looking like his shoes, because that's all he'll be able to see.

'Maybe, this time,' answers Elsbetha, as she reaches for the one Sobranie she allows herself to smoke each week, hating herself for the vestigial habit, but unutterably enslaved to the weed. David didn't know until now about this and is clearly shocked, but knows better than to say anything. The two of them live on tenterhooks and tread on eggshells. If a baby doesn't come soon, their relationship will die. For years the biological clock has been ticking ever louder, so that at times it's deafening, able to blot out the sound even of the big bass bell outside, with its subsonic boom. When she was forty it sounded like Big Ben. By the time she was forty-five it was like the outsize bell in the Kremlin, the Tsar Kolokov, which weighs in mightily at four hundred thousand pounds. For whom does it toll? You guess.

On the asphalt. A body that's made its last movement. CSI taking pictures, of contusion and exit wound, bone debris and precise location. Forensic experts cross and circle like bees around the empty vessel of her brother.

Tierra is eleven years old, too young to see this sort of thing and avoid permanent emotional scarring. This is a terrible image bank to carry with her into adult life, too heavy a load. It's the sort of unshakeable image that will wake her in the night as if she has a car alarm instead of a heart. It will displace all the images of him alive, so very alive. Because he filled his skin, had an energy about him that made the world around him dance.

Her mother has to work to pay the bills, so she can't afford to stay at home and look after Tierra, despite the awfulness of what's happened. She also doesn't feel guilty about this. She's had to immunize herself against guilt. Luckily, Clarisse, the woman next door, is willing to mind Tierra while her mother goes off to one of her jobs, in Lucky's. To make ends meet she has to moonlight as well, so works from home as a cab despatcher, with calls routed through to her from eleven until two.

The cops who came to see them as a family were wearied by asking the standard questions to people made numb by grief, sitting on threadbare sofas in dowdy apartment blocks. Questions about young men wearing bling and often sporting colours. Young men blasted away in the night. No, Antony had no enemies. No, he was not aligned with any gang. No, he didn't use drugs and he didn't sell drugs, other than some weekends when he'd smoke marijuana. Tierra's mother thought it better to be upfront about everything and, anyway, all of Antony's friends smoked dope. She thought nothing of it herself. It was a generational thing.

The mother's voice is hoary with cigarette smoke and tiredness and an emptiness which seemed to grip her womb. Her only son. Lost to her. His voice. Those eyes. That way he had of teasing her almost like a lover.

When she phoned Antony's father to break the news to him, the old goat's latest paramour, Cristabel, told her he'd gone to Mexico for a few days. She didn't have to ask anything else. This was no vacation in Cozumel. He'd have left with a few blocks of dollar bills wrapped in Ziplocs. A few days after he returned to the US some fantastically weary Mexican drug mules would cross the hard desert from Tijuana or Nogales with bundles of marijuana on their backs. Men, women, often children bearing their shrink-wrapped parcels. Nu Nu had had a fantastic role model in his father.

'Tell him his son's been killed . . . and remind him that his name was Antony. In case it's slipped his mind.'

Mrs Doon replaces the phone in its cradle. She hates Cristabel: she always uses her best cyanide voice when talking to her. Her, with her unblemished skin and obsession with working out. That flat belly of Cristabel's well-nigh bloody kills her. She pats her own soft belly, the rubberiness around her navel.

The spermatozoon race was the one that enthralled Elsbetha. Life's most dynamic competition, she thought. She imagined them in the warm Gulf Stream of her insides, swimming purposefully, so many tiny versions of David – thrashing without knowing why toward their ultimate aim. Primitive desire, genetic instinct, moving on through warm liquid. Haploid cells able to create a zygote in the womb, a single cell with a full set of chromosomes which can grow into an embryo. Reaching her ovum's safe harbour.

She's almost a specialist herself now, knowing everything about the journey, able to visualize the little tadpoles with their tiny heads and their tails so very small – only fifty microns would you believe – all racing to fertilize one egg. That's all it takes. Please God let it be her one egg. Making her feel like a true woman. Making sense of her body. Keeping her biological line from snapping off into oblivion.

Come on, you blind hapless creatures on your way to somewhere or certain death! For Christ's sake. Follow the pheromonal signs. Past Scylla and Charybdis, the rock and the whirlpool within her.

So many will be killed: a silent genocide taking place; sacrifice, deaths by drowning. This is how you create a baby.

And if one of the hapless ones does make it through it'll have to negotiate the cumulus cells and then the zona pellucida – obstacles, walls, an impossible array of obstacles along the way.

But one has to make it through. That was the considered opinion – and expensive considered opinion of the curiously named Dr Sardonicus (highly recommended by all and sundry, despite the name). He is talking options with David and Elsbetha. In the file open before him on the desk is all manner of information about the two of them. Timetables of ovulation. Medical confessions. Probing questions that reach into the deepest intimacies.

Outside the clinic a monstrously dimensioned limousine passes by, carrying a sharp-suited crew of men headed to meet some mules who have brought new dope via Santa Barbara and Monterey. The world of coincidence is uncharted mystery. Cities abound with it.

After their visit to the clinic, the fruitless couple are mute. They have already raised a second mortgage to pay for the fees and their meal together is a mixture of sullen silence and annoyance with each other. Elsbetha imagines her body going through a period of desertification, sharp-spined cactus breaking through the skin of her legs, her belly flaking at first before cracking like clay under a baking sun. And this waking nightmare is clear, too clear, too, well, skewed towards reality. The cacti are like the ones she saw growing out of crumbly rock formations in the Joshua Tree National Park – claret cup and beavertail. Her skin is a painful membrane under an aggressive sun. That sun which looks like a sacramental wafer, hanging as a pale disk in the sky, but changing as it rises towards noon height, threatening to flamethrower each and every plant into a shrivelled twig. In the cloying silence of their duplex, David and Elsbetha are paralysed by inability. In turn, guilt racks each one, even as Elsbetha gives in to vivid hallucinations so rabid that they could match St Anthony's. It is as if she, too, is stranded between the Nile and Red Sea, rather than in a barely humidified duplex as the sun really begins to cook up. Her pain is of Old Testament proportions. David wanders from room to room, lost, confused, unmanned.

All because one miserable sperm isn't able to make it through! Elsbetha has threatened to leave him over it. She has kept her meticulous calendar, she has eaten good food, stayed off all bar one cigarette each week. As she's tracked her interior seasons and lived by the thermometer, she has succumbed to feeling unwomanned. So, an unwoman and an unman live together in a duplex. She wants a baby, more than breath itself. He can't deliver. Not a recipe for conjugal bliss, you wouldn't have thought.

David dons his coat obediently.

Even though La Taqueria – which is right next to the BART station – is full of people and a rumbustious after work hubbub, Elsbetha's voice comes across as like that of a jobbing actor failing to declaim Shakespeare, loud but with the words slightly garbled. Nevertheless he is able to hear each and every one of his failings meticulously outlined. She spares no blushes. She spits out scorn at his lazy sperm and points at his manhood with her newly manicured fingers, directing her venom. She tells him how he hasn't been the same ever since starting the new job, working with all those nightmare kids such that she hardly knows him anymore. What basis is that to keep him as a lover? A lover with a rubber hose between his legs, lifeless and pathetically long.

'It's not the kids who are nightmarish, just the world they inhabit,' counters David, who will not give in to her over this point. He treasures the students. There are days when he thinks to himself that even if he can't have children himself that he will look after these other kids, nurture them, show them that the world isn't all made up of hurt. His wife has been given enough time to build up a head of steam.

'Funny how you can address other people's problems but not your own . . . I've had enough, David. You are the most pathetic specimen of manhood and our life together is just horrible. If you can call this lustreless existence a life. Do you know what it's like to wither on the vine? Do you? Of course not. You don't understand anything. You're just surplus to requirements. You're just a waste of a skin.'

This was a more vitriolic attack than any he remembered and there was something about her demeanour which suggested that this time she really was at breaking point. Her eyes had a purple glow. Her hands agitated the flatware. She had vented her spleen and there was a hint of satisfaction about her. David's mind had drifted, trying to identify the music playing on the radio. Ozomatli, perhaps. His wife was far away now, stranded on a separate continent. The boundaries of their marriage had once again shifted, so that she was almost out of reach. There she was on an ice floe, seemingly content there in her cold isolation, the water between them the colour of grey slate. Their marriage was glacial, with no sign of thaw.

Tierra has a Tinkerbell bag on her back and in her pocket she carries a mobile phone, a startlingly pink affair with the face of a cartoon princess emblazoned on it. The school bus is early and Luther, who's been driving this route each morning for over twenty years, flashes her a sudden smile, mainly in order to show off his new teeth, which cost him a fortune on a payment plan that will take him up to seventy-five years of age to clear. That, coupled with the fact that he likes the little girl and feels deeply upset about what has happened to her. There are too many wanton homicides in this city he thinks, too much stupid waste.

On the bus Tierra stares at the phone but she doesn't have anyone to ring anymore and so, almost without thinking, she scribbles RIP Ant and Monte like an automaton over and over on the blue covers of her school books. Tierra thinks back to the black-and-yellow tape. For her it represents the boundary between her childhood and this new hell.

There once was a charming princess who always wore the same primrose-coloured dresses. She was warned never ever to go to the Wild Wood where the Ferocious Creatures lived. She didn't want to, and was very scared about it, but something compelled her to set one foot after another over the twigs that crackled like brushfire. Bound that way. And the edge of the wood is where the bad things start. And on she goes, fearful and fearless at one and the same time. Beyond the boundary.

Tierra's school stands on a little hillock. On one side there is an unkempt park which is only slightly less dangerous by day than it is at night, when you'd have to be the Devil himself to take a saunter. On the other side stands a community of low-income homes which are so closely packed together that in the distance the roofs have the appearance of corrugated cardboard. There are some buildings which look like an East German army barracks, and that's a suitable comparison in a sense, as they probably need an army to tame things around here, where every moment is a flashpoint, where every discarded beer can might as well be a powder keg. It's life in wartime, where the neighbours are planning acts of secession and takeover. Don't trust anyone. Don't make pacts. If someone stops to say hello keep on walking. Unless they seem to have money. In which case do make a pact with them so that you and your friends can rob them in relative safety.

Keynote High is in no-man's-land. But every pupil in the school knows a 'soldier' or at least someone who's been hurt in the fighting. It's dystopian hereabouts, with burned-out cars making the whole place look like the set of a John Carpenter movie. The local hospital specializes in gunshot wounds, and even the experienced staff there are surprised that they manage to save so many, especially when the victims have been drilled with bullets, riddled with bleeding holes. In this they are not dissimilar to Northern Ireland: some hospitals during the Troubles became astonishingly adept at dealing with dreadful injuries, men who'd been punished by the terrorists, who discharged shotguns into their kneecaps.

Not that many miles away from the school stand the new yuppie homes built on land which once used to house the great naval dockyards with their grey armadas. Here the sun never sets on the Hotel Mundial without the bar being absolutely full of elegant creatures, flitting from table to table, sipping margaritas. Outside, Royal terns arrow-dive into the surf. The shops hereabouts are repositories of expensive design. Mascot. Delibes. Sorrento. The women talk about designer brands they covet as the tequila makes them more loquacious. From the verandah you can see grey whales making their way from balmy Mexican waters to Alaskan wild seas. Sometimes they go unnoticed, as if they have no value. No more than a handbag.

But that's a world away from Tierra's school. In the last few weeks one of the students saw a man hold a gun against his mother's head before raping her in front of him. Another girl had to step over a dead gang member to get to school on time. As three boys waited for the bus one morning they witnessed two men shooting at each other and were glad they weren't caught in the crossfire. The bullets zinged. The men ran away. The boys went to their lessons.

On his desk David had an incomplete list of violent offences in the school district going back six months, which he had been perusing in a vainglorious attempt to understand what the hell was going on. He could feel the pressure building all around. Students brought the anxieties and brutality of their home lives into the classroom, so you could judge by the dew of sweat on their skin that the neighbourhood was simmering. And how. David kept in constant contact with the police and social services in case anyone needed grief counselling when they returned to school. Form an orderly queue.

Tierra's was the sixth grade but within weeks of her brother's death some of her teachers were asking whether she should stay there. Not just in that grade but in any classroom, as she'd become a crazy firecracker, as disruptive as a swarm of hornets. Her temper seemed hot enough in itself to burn the school down.

She chased after one boy and hit him in the eye with her fist. Admittedly he'd said something to provoke her but as he recoiled from her first assault she started to rain blows upon him with a frenzy that astonished onlookers. They could only feel relieved that she didn't have anything harder than her fists to hit him with. She was a dervish with flailing arms.

'I'm going to kill you, you little fuck.' Tierra, the little princess, uttered the words with a chill sincerity.

So the girl with the pink bag was now completely objectionable. Her work had gone from being carefully arranged to non-existent. She challenged student and teacher alike and had no deference to authority. In fact she didn't seem to recognize her place in the world. Her concentration was gone. Her self-image had diminished to zero.

Some of the teachers failed to remember what had happened to her while others had so cauterized their emotions that they did not allow themselves to remember. They could only defend themselves against the horror of the job by not caring about anything or anyone other than themselves. So they forgot her pain, her loss, her daylight nightmares full of tarpaulin and police tape.

Rationally, they had a duty to the other kids. One or two still wanted to read a book, wanted to achieve good grades, even though half of those even had seen things too grisly or menacing to put in a film. There are invisible bullets that leave no trace other than in one's imaginings, dark hunks of metal lodged in the brain that become septic.

Trauma in this school was worse than soldiers returning from Iraq, or from fighting the Taliban. Violence was quotidian. It was as casual as putting on clothes, part of the weft and weave of the day-to-day. And Tierra was a roadside bomb, quietly dangerous, set to blow you apart. Just a little girl. Loaded with Semtex.

Sometimes Tierra expresses it all as one long curse that spills out of her mouth like a witch's spell. The words come out in a spray of spit and rage. Eventually.

David adds more soft furnishings to his room, attempts to soften the impression that this is room for interrogation. He has been listening to Tierra's complicated thoughts, made urgent by her rage, and taking copious notes. He writes down even the most casual detail so that he can sift through it looking for clues when he has some peace and quiet. He might be in his grave before that happens.

This is their first session. She is hyper-attentive and suspiciously watchful, a mongoose eyeing up a cobra.

She is still ranting – about what she is going to do to anyone who looks at her In The Wrong Way. She'll kill him, she says unequivocally. She weighs 110 pounds and is barely five foot high and in her head she's no pint-sized would-be murderer. She is right and the world is wrong. It's that simple.

'We don't have to speak at all,' said David, setting the file down, and placing his biro in his pocket.

There was a long silence, brooding with threat. He offered her a piece of chocolate, doubting whether mongooses liked chocolate. Tierra studiously refused to look at him, choosing to stare aimlessly out of the window. She didn't say a word, her little lips zipped. Finally it was time to conclude the session. David thanked her for her presence, without a hint of irony. Surprisingly the little girl looked pleased by his gesture, as if she'd actually enjoyed the company, or the attention. David had grown used to unexpected gestures. There was no textbook about this stuff, and certainly no rulebook.

After the little girl left the room, David opened her file and started to read the terrible story of her short life. Even couched in the language of officialdom it was the sort of biography that might have crushed her soul already, were it not for the fact that Tierra had mettle. She had already confided a lot in some of his colleagues. Maybe said it all. David doubted it somehow. A brother's death changed everything, deadened all sunshine.

She had been an exemplary pupil all along – her homework handed in punctually and her behaviour in class winning her stars every week. She was an extrovert at home, her mother describing her in one interview as a ladleful of sunshine. Her brother was her constant target – he who must be teased – and she had a rare skill at winding him up, especially when he was in his girl-chasing phase. She used to try to catch him at intimate moments; in his room, with cheerleaders.

She was the one who gave him the nickname Nu Nu. David smiled as he read this. He himself had a brother called Jonathan and he always called him Do Do, dating back to the time when he was a year and a half or so and couldn't get his mouth around the syllables. The same brother who now lived in Ulan Bator in Mongolia. Couldn't he have found somewhere further away?

Antony is a shadow cast from the grave, over Tierra's life and that of her mother's. At home the mother's face is set in the rictus of grief and she now chain smokes from dusk until dawn. Tierra doesn't know that her mother escapes in many other ways, through pipes of crack and crystal meth, all she can find on the street. *She needs to anaesthetize her grief,* said one report on David's desk, quoting her own description of *the emptiness in her womb. Cried for nine days,* it continued, her ribs hurting from her shuddering sobs. Before withdrawing into a conch shell of chemicals and alcohol, dealing with his absence by getting absent.

Reading the transcripts of some of the other interviews in the reports was painful because of what they said about the way the mother's brain was dismantled. She described how she left Tierra alone one day to buy a rock from a Chicano who worked a corner near the Tienda Roja, leaving Tierra to her own devices in the house. She couldn't have been gone for more than ten minutes but when she returned her daughter was stabbing out the eyes of her favourite teddy bear, digging into its face with the sharp handle of a plastic comb. Exacting revenge.

Little wonder, then, that this girl is so combative in class, answering her teachers back, out of control, sharp tongued, fractious. David knows he is her last chance; that she's close to being thrown out of school. But he can see a glimmer, the tiniest glister of hope.

By their fourth session David is ready to ask her about the fateful day. He knows he runs the risk of bringing it all back in floods, the sheer *vividness* of her brother's death. For some of the children a loud voice, a police siren, even seeing an object the colour of blood can trigger the most overwhelming flashbacks, leaving them shivering like drenched puppies. Panic, rage, fear, all in a cocktail. David pre-empts all of these, talking about the way in which you can forget by remembering, by knowing where you bury the bad memories, by unearthing them. And the little girl talks, bringing the dark creatures to the surface. She walks with him into the wood.

When David started on this sort of work, his first case was so testing he had to receive therapy himself in order to deal with the magnitude of the pain, real off-the-graph stuff. Tierra reminds him of that other girl, who had lemur-like dark rings of sleeplessness around her eyes. Who had a soul in torment, writhing and thrashing like a conger eel.

That poor unfortunate, Maxine, had lived with a monster of a father: when she was five he had set one of the beds in the house on fire in the twisted hope that he would kill everyone under its roof. She remembered the firemen in their yellow hats and the acrid tang of smoke in her nostrils. A couple of years later health workers found tiny cockroaches in her ears. When she was nine she witnessed her brother being stabbed in the back and, not surprisingly, by the time she was ten she was exhibiting a raft of symptoms of Post-Traumatic Stress Disorder. So, this, a childhood. Police cars, fire tenders, syringes and bugs would cause her to feel total fear. It took three years even to begin to help her properly.

But Tierra is different. David senses that from the start. At the outset of their therapy she exhibits some sort of calm, and even though she is prone to wild flare-ups of anger she is able to rein it in, be self-possessed, to sit there without fidgeting recklessly. She isn't hyper. But perhaps that's because her own emotions have subdued her. Today she sits stranded, marooned on a small island of anxiety in the slough of despond. But the craft is at least still and settled in position.

'Mom went to play bingo last night,' she volunteered, after the silence had begun to worry at her.

'Your mother likes bingo?'

David realized the stupidity of the question as soon as he'd asked.

'She doesn't stay long and she never, ever wins anything, well, sometimes ten dollars. She goes up the street, just one stop on the bus and she always thought that she'd be safe, and we'd be safe, as she was only a short distance away. She'd never go out without Nu Nu being there to keep me company.

'And he was . . ?'

'He always was. Without fail. He was always there for me, even when I knew he had better things to do than hang about with his kid sister watching dumb-ass movies. But he knew we lived in a dangerous place and that he could never leave me alone. So, as I said, he was always there. If the forest was dark he had a bright light to

97

banish away the shadows. He was just a bright light, you know?'

David noted the elegant expressions. He wrote them on a yellow legal pad, which at least was beginning to fill up. A dark forest. A bright light.

'And what was special about last night's bingo game?'

'Mom had just started her second game when men came in wearing masks. They all had guns and one of them was waving his around like mad, as if he was drunk, or mad or something. They took money from everyone. Mom couldn't believe it, what with what happened to Nu Nu and all.'

The little girl froze with expectation as she finished, then she relaxed a little, hunching in her shoulders and lifting her knees up to her chest. Defensive. Scared. But not as frightened as she'd been.

'What if I shared a story with you?' asked David with a smile, offering her three See's Candies from a one pound box. But she refused.

David pressed on with his tale. About a girl a little younger than Tierra, who lived in Minnesota.

The girl's name was Betty Campbell, and the name of the town was Larkspur, and every day she would ask the meaning of this and the meaning of that, asking endless questions of the postman and the man who cleaned the windows and the one in green overalls who tended gardens, and her parents of course, who often felt under siege. *Why? What? When? What exactly? What if?* The questions came as if off a Gatling gun. Everyone she met was probed and tested for what they knew about things, knew about stuff. *Why do you clean windows? Who gives you the letters? Why is snow white? What's the name of the fastest animal in the world?*

'A cheetah,' said the postman, happily, thinking of the sleek leopard of the savannah, swiftly creeping up on a Thomson's gazelle. This was the first time he'd been able to answer one of Betty's general knowledge questions. He beamed with pride. And he knew the answer to *who gives you the letters?*

'The woman in the mail office,' he said, his heart racing as if he was an accelerating cheetah, as he conjured up a vision of Patrice, who ran the place. He fell more deeply in love with her with every grey gunny sack of letters she lifted out from behind the counter. One day, not that far into the future, he would marry her and, in time, their son Mickey would leave Stanford University with a degree in astrophysics and get himself a job working in a post office. Despite the fact that this decision would mortify his parents, they would know better than to ask him to rethink. He would have done enough thinking for one lifetime. Worked out the answer to a significant question about antimatter that Betty would have liked, had she understood it.

'Snow is white so we can distinguish it from soot,' said Bill Drabkin the farmer, a man with a head shaped like a turnip who leaned over the gate to confide in the little girl. He also explained how every snowflake gathered around a tiny, tiny piece of dust, and together they paused for an astonished moment to consider how such a perfect thing could indeed gather around a smidgeon of soot.

Betty was like a question factory, with a production line that couldn't stop. Everyone liked her despite her persistence, in part because of her enthusiasm, her delight in acquiring encyclopaedic knowledge. Because once she knew something she never forgot it. You could test her: she'd never be found wanting. The answer you gave her stayed with her.

By day Betty was the prime interrogator, the small inquisitor. But at night she was a different kettle of fish altogether. Because Betty Campbell was scared of the moon. Petrified of its glaucous orb. Moonophobic. Selenophobic, to give it its correct title. Like a girl's name. Scary Selena. Up there, terrifyingly.

Now, Betty was sufficiently aware that there was nothing to be scared of. The moon wasn't going to come crashing through the roof if it blew a gale. But she also knew that phobias didn't make sense and that her feelings of terror were as real to her as the rain pattering against the window: the fear gripped her deep within. She knew of other phobias, people who were scared of water, gold, blood and handcuffs. But they didn't know why. The hard man scared of the minute spider in the bath. The woman petrified of wooden spoons. Honestly. Keep her out of the kitchen or you'll have a madwoman on your hands, screaming as she hacks away in the air with the nearest knife within reach. (You can kill spoons, for they do bleed, the same as enemies. She knows.)

Should there be a moon at any stage, from a slivery crescent to one as round as a cheese, Betty could be found shivering under the bed. This fear plagued her for a whole year, despite all the folk remedies and therapies her parents tried in order to solve the problem of the fearful nights. Then one night her father talked to her, giving her a full explanation . . .

'Once upon a time all the creatures of the world lived in fear of the night, from the smallest scurrying mouse, all the birds of the air, the burrowing badgers, the startled deer, the tiger, the morning cockerel – each and every one living in abject fear of the night and what it might bring. Once the sun set behind the mountains, as it did behind Mount Mishap which overlooks the town, or made its descent behind the trees, or lowered itself as if *into* the plains, a dread would settle over them all. All animal life would quake, all avian life tremble its feathers, as they tried to settle, to stay still.

'Then, one day the Great Goddess of Creation, Kooch, asked them all if they'd like to be awake at night. To become part of a new legion of nocturnal creatures.

'For many animals and birds, the idea of being awake to the terrors of the night was truly a nightmare, but others had such unwavering faith in the Great Creator that they would have willingly travelled to the far ends of the earth at Her bidding. They were only too ready to become nocturnal in their habits, if She thought it fit. But before changing the order of things, She created a lamp from an old piece of wrinkled paper in her pocket, on which were written instructions She had received from her mother all those aeons ago: "How to create crawlers, flying creatures and animals with four limbs and so on".

'She cut out a circle of parchment using her fine silver

scissors and tossed it into the air on a graceful arc of arm swing. It drifted up, as if gravity didn't matter, or hadn't yet been proposed. It finally got snagged in the space between two stars (the Great Creator had deliberately set nets of light between them, when she had invented galaxies the previous week) and instantly it began to reflect sunlight as the earth curved towards it. The paper turned into a moon and the moon into a shining lamp – a beacon to lead tired travellers, a benificent moon to light the elegant dances of a myriad moths: the snowberry clearwing, the white-plagued sphinx, the clover looper and the oleander hawk.

'The pearl-coloured orb and its reflected light became a source of sustenance to spectral plants, and they grew towards it, their stems silvery, their leaves corruscating with flecks of moonlight that caught on tiny hairs on their upper sides. The light filtered even to the forest floor or hedge base. So tiny, twitching shrews could see clearly as they sought midnight feasts of scattered seeds, and owls could float by on hushed wings, and three-toed sloths could dream of finding luscious grapes hanging heavily among jungle lianas and vines.'

And with that, Betty's father drew open the curtains to show her that you could still see the folds in the ancient paper, reminding his daughter of the way in which the Great Creator placed the moon as both gift and blessing, to banish fears and illuminate dark corners. He pointed out the craters like pockmarks on its face and suggested it must be a teenage moon, and they both laughed at that, until Betty realized that she was staring at the moon without a quiver in her heart and it was then that she hugged her father as if she was trying to press the breath out of him and they both sat still on the bed, revelling in the sight of its creamy balloon.

'It's now my favourite lamp,' she told her father, with a steady voice born of the bravery that was newly hatched within her. And she hugged him again, feeling safer now than she could ever imagine, breathing in the smell of stale tobacco on his cardigan and the slightly lemony tang of pomade in his hair. Marvellous Tobacco No 1 was the make, long since discontinued. A connection with his grandfather, one of Marvellous' all-time faithful customers. He stored the cigarettes in brown Kilner jars, wrapped in cotton wool, in case of plague or outbreak of war.

'And I have a secret to share with you, Tierra,' said David. 'That's a true story, inasmuch as these things can ever be true. I did change the name, but that's what happened to me. My father told me that story and it banished so many fears. Because I was as scared of the moon as anyone can be. But since he told me the tale I now enjoy the night, absolutely revel in it and like nothing better than walking in redwoods when the world is impossibly still, which allows you to listen to the crackle and scurry of small mammals, all the unfamiliar sounds. I've gone so far as to take up astrononomy – I know the names of maybe a hundred other moons, and I've seen them too. Enceladus. Deimos. Charon. Puck.'

Tierra looked at him, staring into his eyes as if she was facing him down.

'So I want to help banish your fears.'

And with that Tierra moved an inch towards him.

Circumspect and still wary but nevertheless an inch forward, which, for her, was tantamount to a full-blown migration. And then she wept, and David joined in and you'd have been hard pressed to work out who was gushing the most tears as they both had depths of pain to plumb. He cried for his unborn son. The girl's shirt was wet by the time she composed herself and David had to wipe his nose in his sleeve.

And that was another therapy session over. David was wiped out by it, emotionally. He had never revealed himself before, or confided more in his client than the client had in him. Shocked by his complete lack of professionalism he watched as Zukie, Tierra's new friend, walked her to the school gates and then home.

Tierra could barely keep up with her friend's excited chatter as she gossiped about boys and girls and music. She was glad of the company. The way home always seemed to take a long time when she walked by herself. That had as much to do with Nu Nu not being there to welcome her home as it was to do with the weariness she felt, having seen too much and grown up too quickly. She was also thinking of Betty and how she'd befriended the girl in the story, grown close to her as David talked about her fears. A riot of questions, she was. And lived in a town of good people. With a father who cared for her deeply. What a fantasy!

That night, David had arranged to meet his wife in an Asian small plate restaurant on the corner of College and Alcatraz. Nowadays he needed his negotiating skills outside of work, as his wife burned in a sulphurous rage at the very thought of David and his myriad inadequacies, as she saw them. Tonight she wasn't angry, just sour, and he imagined her spittle to be a tad hydrochloric.

'What sort of day did you have?' he asked, with the temerity of someone treading round a pit viper.

'Oh, I just sat around at home and stared into the abyss. There was nothing on TV to watch and not a living thing to distract me. Loneliness can be toxic, eat away at your marrow. It's tough being dead, David. Dead on the inside.'

David wanted to point out pedantically that his wife was alive, but she'd have seen that as provocation. He decided to avoid the hazard. She was hell-bent on wallowing. She wallowed in misery, was its codependent.

'What it is to be a barren woman. A living desert.'

David could feel a sandy grit between his teeth. He saw air from outside blowing the candles of the other diners. A desert wind blowing through.

'I was designed to carry and bear children, and now all I have to do with all those inherent skills, all that toughness and innate care, is wistfully turn the pages of *People* magazine and register all the photographs of all those people being happy. All the film stars wih their truckloads of children being happy, David. With their fucking children, David. Take that Angelina Jolie. She'll need to get a second truck the way she's going. How many has she got again?'

David downed the rest of his wine in one. It was going to be a long evening. When his wife was in one of these moods it was best to locate the bunker.

'You've destroyed me, David. You and your failure. You and your clinical inadequacies. Your pathetic reproductive apparatus. Which disgusts me, by the way. You're only half a man and you'll forgive me if I sneer at you. A poor excuse, that's what you are, a poor excuse.'

She lifted her glass to give her something to brandish. But then, unexpectedly, she started to snort and cry, so loudly that all the other diners turned to look then turned back again. Elsbetha convulsed in her misery. Her sobbing could gain an Oscar and even though David had been on the receiving end of so much emotional fakery, this time he knew it was true. Elsbetha shuddered and convulsed. She was breaking down in front of him, and despite his oh-too-ample experience he was helpless to alleviate her pain, to even come close to it.

Elsbetha left for the bathroom, and while she was gone David ordered food even though he wasn't authorized to do so. It was something he used to joke about – who wore the trousers in their marriage – but now he couldn't take so much as a breath without sanction. She was emasculating him, that was for sure. It might seem callous or unfeeling to order the food, but it was a way of holding on to some semblance of normality about the evening. The hors d'oeuvres arrived before his wife came back and so he began to pick at the calamari absent-mindedly. The batter was light, the sea tang satisfying, the Sicilian lemons exquisitely tart. He felt a pang of guilt about these small pleasures as he knew his wife was in a very dark place. But he wasn't the one to help her. She probably genuinely hated him by now.

As he slowly cleared the plate – inviting all the avenging wrath of Elsbetha – he started defiantly enjoying the prawns in palm sugar and the pre-eminently spicy wontons. As he did so he tried to imagine what would be on Tierra's menu this evening. She didn't live quite on the wrong side of the tracks where there were children suffering from rickets even in this day and age, but in common with most of the kids in the city she was on a high-sugar, maxi-fat diet, though in her case she burned it off with her carnival of nervous tics. How cynical they were, thought David, thinking of the rapacious companies with their avaricious shareholders who lined their pockets on the proceeds of obesity. It was all so beautifully packaged, with astronauts and Disney sanctions. The trans fat was the wrong sort of fat but it reached the shelves backed by accompanying TV ads. Cheesy Freezies. McKeen's Arizona Home Fries. Teri's Chicken Isits. Big Monster Chews. Some children lived on Cheerios, without milk. He knew this for a fact. Two dry bowlfuls a day.

When his wife returned she seemed to have left the spitting viper behind in the restroom. She even actually looked as if she wanted to enjoy the evening, even though she gave his cleared plate the evil eye. Luckily David had had the foresight to order exactly the same round again and let his wife enjoy the little delicacies. And as the minutes passed it did seem that she had genuinely buried the hatchet, or called a truce or something. By the time the coffees arrived David had grown weary of her fixed smile, the one that was hiding something he couldn't properly comprehend. It unsettled him. It really unsettled him.

Tierra noticed that he wasn't really there, that David's mind was wandering. He was attentive enough on the surface – taking notes, engaging with her at every turn, and looking helpless as a newborn baby every time she eluded him, slipped away from his grasp. She was mercury, skidding across white tiles as tiny metallic pearls. A comet racing.

In their weekly sessions there were still times of combat, when Tierra gave vent to anger. He could best describe it as volcanic, the pressure building up until something has to blow. Sometimes she was just sullenly silent and at times like those he fixed her with an eagle eye, often impatient with her, needing her to settle down. But those moments were most infrequent now. Mostly they just sat and looked at each other, or talked about ordinary things. They talked weather, about garbage on the streets, and boys. Tierra was taking an interest in boys all of a sudden.

'What's up, Doc?' she asked him out of the blue one day.

David didn't reply, partly because he felt as if he hadn't slept for a decade or more. He had panda eyes, an Old Testament beard in the making, edged in grey, and hair like an electrified scarecrow. He felt as old as Methuselah, as if the world had been hanging from his shoulders and the corrosive effect of the years had been whittled away at the very crag of his existence.

'I'm so sorry, Tierra,' he said in a voice thick with fatigue. I have problems at home and I'm afraid I've brought them in here with me. It's the most terribly unforgivable thing I can do when the whole point of this is to help you cope with things, but there, I've done it and I can only say I'm sorry for letting you down so badly.'

'It's alright. I forgive you.'

David was brought up short by that word. It was the one they'd been circling around these past months, but *rage* and *revenge* and *hatred* and so many others that glowed in the red part of the emotional spectrum had obscured it from view. He'd been following his own masterclass in forgiveness as he tried to forget all the spat words, the acid spittle of his wife, who had grown really vicious now, as if the very point of her life was to erode his self-esteem down to a bare nub and then erase that with a flourish. But he had to deal with it. He still loved her. And her spleen was born of a terrible thing that was being wrought on her, an aching, expanding emptiness that grew to fill all her thoughts. And now this little girl, this brave little girl was forgiving him, for forgetting to leave Elsbetha behind him as he walked into their therapy room. If there was one thing certain to annihilate all sense of self-worth it was this.

'Thank you, Tierra.'

The girl's body language was expressive now, a complicated set of gestures, with a hint of burgeoning sexuality mixed in with the pain and anger. She was almost too close. Her shoulders dropped a little as she shed her stress.

And then she began to speak, an unbridled, unrestrained rivulet of words, ideas tumbling out of her as she tried to tell him what she really felt, and his pen couldn't keep up, and he cursed himself for not getting new batteries for his

109

recorder, but then again this was the therapy, this word river with its furious eddies and verbal rapids of rage. The words spumed as if they were crashing against rocks. Her thin arms flailed in a frenzy. She listed the hopes she used to have, all dashed by that bullet. And listed ways she'd changed, how she wanted out so often, to get out of this life with its pain and promise of more pain. And mixed with it all were the abandoned dreams of a young girl in an inner city. How she'd wanted to be a dancer, a poet, an artist living in a Brooklyn brownstone. To be on *American Idol*. Any life that wasn't as hollow and pointless as her mother's life, with its deadening rituals of bingo, drugs and endless TV, and most of all that punishing lack of love. And David was amazed by the eloquence of it all, the loquacity leavened by rank pain and ferocious memory. She knew, she told him, how this school couldn't educate her all the way to where she wanted to go, but then again she knew that the librarian would get her pretty much any book she asked for, for the simple reason that she was the only student in the school who darkened the library doors; which was a crying shame because she'd learned how to escape there. To Balzac's France and Hardy's England. These were remote geographies she knew well. And she liked Agatha Christie, Charles Dickens – especially *Bleak House* – and James Joyce and his *Dubliners* and all the stories of the Greeks. She listed them almost with apology, knowing that in this place it made her more of a freak show than a girl whose brother had been gunned down. And Victor Hugo. She loved Victor Hugo. 'He was a peach of a writer and his books were awesome.' David was flabbergasted. He had known nothing of her reading. He must be a complete and utter moron.

'Before Nu Nu died I had planned my life,' Tierra continued. 'I had plotted as much of it as I could, and before you say anything I know I'm too young for that sort of thing, but that's the way I am and I thought nothing would change that. I used to think that other people's lives were so, well, messy, so all over the place, so I had to make plans. All the time, plans for this, plans for that. Take my mother, for instance. She doesn't know where anything is, and we don't have that much to begin with, so how on earth she can go and lose so many things goodness only knows. The house is always in disarray and Nu Nu always used to say (with his name she crosses herself in the Catholic way, even though she and her family go to the African Evangelical Chruch, where the choir sings like the Ronettes) that our house was haywire.'

The young girl drew some deep breaths, as if she were inhaling the last inch of a cigarette.

'But all the dreaming and plotting and planning came to an end when he died.' (She crossed herself again, automatically.) 'Everything came to an end that day.'

'What has that done to you? What do you think about now?'

'Revenge. All of the time, revenge.'

'Just that?'

'Just that.'

Outside, the morning fog dissipated and David could see the Richmond Bridge revealed in the far distance, and in the sky, the main of light. It was a landscape lit for an epiphany maybe. A fine day, whatever. Children playing in the schoolyard sounded like any other kids and there was no hint in the hubbub of how tough things were for them, and how relentless the challenges.

From some parked cars came the sonic thuds of hip hop and he knew there'd be police keeping an eye on them after the last spate of drug dealing to under twelves. Under twelves! These were children who wouldn't know how to spell what they were taking. Growing up too fast. Talking of motherfucker this and motherfucker that and talk of Kalashnikovs and songs about M1 carbines taking the place of songs about growing up, fairytale stuff, all the stories of an innocent world that would be as strange to them as a walk in Madagascar.

'Is there anything else I can do to help?' asked David.

Tierra answered in a beat. She had been waiting for this moment, breath duly bated.

'I want to go and see the Woman-Who-Sleeps, the one who arrived in a paper boat. More than anything else in the whole wide world. Can we, oh please, can we?'

Tierra was referring to the arrival of Flavia in her craft, an event which had caused an enormous stir. The news channels had already started to refer to her as the Woman-Who-Sleeps.

'That's a great idea. I've been meaning to go see her myself.'

He would feel like a father taking his daughter out on a trip. He decided to send Tierra's mother a note asking for her permission forthwith. They would go to see the Woman-Who-Sleeps.

It was the coastguard who first spotted her, out there in the channel, beyond the snaggle-toothed chain of islets, beyond the floating acres of kelp where sea otters gambolled, eating the freshest clams on their upturned bellies as they floated on their backs.

The coastguard were detailed to look for boats carrying human cargo – Filipinos in the main – with the crammed stowaways taking the place of red snapper and barracuda in the holds of the fishing boats. The previous week they had stopped a goddam sampan, which looked as if it had come all the way from Hong Kong Harbour. Couldn't have been more than twelve foot long. A lemon sun rose above a calm sea, and there were plenty of whales and dolphins breaking the surface, breaching and skimming the waves. A good day for business on the high seas.

Lieutenant Olivero was the man who caught sight of it – a black spot in the distance – but through his high-grade Zeiss binoculars he could see that there were sharks threshing about it, as if it was carrying a cargo of seal's blood. Yet there was something about the way these great whites were behaving that captured his attention. He knew how they normally behaved when they were in for the kill, building up from cruising speed to attack velocity and it wasn't at all like this. They were more excited this time. This was a mad frenzy of sharks, their olfactories working overtime, their fins scything through water made mad with their collective excitement. And yet they didn't attack. They just surrounded the boat, almost custodial in their attention.

'Hard about!' ordered Captain Evans after Olivero

explained what he could see, or what he thought he could see. Evans, who read too many historical novels about the sea, liked saying *hard about*, stuff like that. Ten minutes later the eight crew members were staring at the most curious thing the sea had ever thrown up in their experience.

In the small boat lay an old woman, her arms akimbo. The captain was convinced she was dead – how else could they explain why the sharks hadn't turned her over? But yet she looked alive, asleep, unusual. As his men used a gaff to bring her alongside the USS *Sea Falcon* the sharks kept a wary distance, but didn't leave, which in itself was out of character. They wanted to escort this woman who looked as if she was asleep. In fact, Captain Evans, who came from Bargoed in South Wales, would hardly have to pay for another drink for the rest of his mortals, as he regaled men in bars with details of this first encounter, such was his undying belief that the woman's lips had moved, just once, but definitely moved.

And yet every rational bit of him had reasoned against that. This was, after all, deep water, where the seabed dropped away beyond the continental shelf and there was no dry land for many leagues. The sun was an oxyacetylene lamp, burning fiercely, and his men had to drink litres of water each day despite the air con. Yet this curious woman didn't have so much as a drop of water on board.

Bones, the medic on board the *Falcon*, ran a saline drip into her arm even though he could not swear she was alive. She wasn't breathing. There was no pulse. Yet there were no signs of death, either. Everything about her confounded

114

explanation. She was in an in-between place. So Bones ran in a drip as the captain and crew watched on, agog. There was something about the woman that was magical, perplexing. Bones had trained as a neurologist before joining the Coastguard and he just knew this wasn't in any of the textbooks.

The boat was made of paper, to boot! Paper! Both Bones and the captain would have had double embolisms had they known how long she and her paper craft had been in the water. Nineteen months, and she had braved the wild gales of the south Atlantic, passed by flotillas of Patagonian penguins and skirted Tierra del Fuego, going against the current, almost being drawn to land and certain shipwreck somewhere on the coast of Peru. For three months the boat had been taken along by the equatorial current, taken on and on. You had to reach for the lexicon of miracles to find an apposite way of describing what was going on. On her saintly progress.

By the time they reached the harbour again a helicopter from the local news channel KNPX hovered steadily above. The rotors whirred like metallic mosquitos. The news crew had picked up a hint of something unusual by monitoring the emergency channels and were flying as close to the edge of the no fly zone as they could without being hunted down by jets. It wasn't often they heard a Code Red, so they'd scrambled with all haste. Captain Evans had already suggested taking the old lady to Morris Hill Hospital as Bones had an inkling that this would call for more specialist medical input than the Navy Hospital at Hood Point could muster.

Krista Winkle, normally the news anchor, but for what might be a whopper story like this one sidestepping into her other role as chief reporter, would be on the five o'clock bulletin a couple of hours later with the words *Breaking News* flashing with all urgency over her bright yellow windcheater. Her report would be picked up by three dozen associate channels and bought by the big players. Authoritative ABC. Scene-setting CNN. Dastardly FOX. The story would be broadcast coast to coast and there would be so many people tuning in they would coin a term for it – viewer gridlock.

'They're calling it a miracle,' announced Krista, for once so aware of the importance of the story that she forgot to check her hair. 'Thirty miles off the coast of Marin County today the crew of the USS *Sea Falcon* picked up a woman, apparently over seventy years of age, who appeared to be sleeping, or in a coma, in a boat made entirely of paper, out of ordinary newspaper in fact. I've spoken to one of the crew members who said that no one, including the on-board medic, could say for certain whether she was alive or dead. Apparently the woman wasn't breathing, and yet she looked entirely healthy. We do not know how long she'd been at sea, nor where she came from, but we gather there were seemingly no clues on board, although most of the newspapers used in the construction of the boat were Spanish, we think from Argentina. At this stage the authorities aren't giving us more on that, as they say they need more time to explore the boat's origins fully. At the time she was spotted, up to fifteen great white sharks were in the water around the boat and they were said to be behaving entirely out of character. There'll be more on this amazing story in an extended edition of *On The Hour* and a complete update just after the break. So stay tuned for *In The News* with Rad Boquesta, here on KNPX.'

Veteran newsman Kent Lachan's beeper sounded as he was disconnecting his sweating hips from those of a Guatemalan prostitute in a hot pillow joint off Highway 19. As he made a pantomime of donning his trousers, falling over and crashing into the ancient television set, he had no inkling he'd be covering the biggest story of his life that very evening. He would be on a flight to Buenos Aires, where he was destined to break the story that would settle a million disputes. When it came to a big story he was a dog with a bone, worrying at it until he could break it.

By nightfall the woman was in Morris Hill Hospital and the boat had been put into storage, under armed guard. As there was so much interest among the public (there were already more people near the storage bay than the jowly hordes who stood in enormous lines around Red Square to see Lenin's body) they'd had to set up temporary restrooms. It was estimated that something like a hundred and fifty thousand people had arrived within six hours of the first newscasts, even though it had been expressly stated that the boat was out of bounds. There were religious nuts, ambulance chasers, amateur newshounds, out-and-out crazies, boat spotters, Krista Winkle's saddo stalker and extended families bringing picnics.

Within a week the city authorities' makeshift viewing facilities bedded in and a ticketing system was established.

Within a couple of days Tierra was taken in David's car to see the boat. He had stopped in the Genoa Deli on the way and loaded up on as many delicacies as he could fit in the trunk. Tierra noticed he had brought all of her favourite things, things she had mentioned in their sessions. She particularly liked brioches and imagined Victor Hugo eating some on a grand boulevard in Paris on a spring day.

The Texan oil trillionaire Marty Shriver had offered a million dollar reward to anyone who could solve the mystery of the Woman-Who-Sleeps. This wasn't an act of casual largesse or philanthropy. He had his own motives for doing so. He'd already invested half his fortune in making arrangements for him and his wife to be cryogenically preserved, ready for some future date when science could bring them back from the dead. He wanted to love her a little bit more. On the far side.

In a phone conversation with the research director of Cryo Labs 2000 the trillionaire had been told that the longevity and state of preservation of the boat lady could hold invaluable clues for their own research work into understanding ageing, death and what follows. Heartened by this, Marty told his PA to start placing ads for the reward.

In the hospital half a dozen of America's most prominent medical practitioners had convened to discuss the lady's condition. They scanned the data and searched in vain for the right words – hibernation, suspended animation, catatonia. They searched in vain because hers was a limbo as yet undescribed. To look at her you'd have to say she was alive: her skin looked like you'd expect an

118

elderly woman's skin to look, but there was no oxygen in her blood and her circulation seemed to have stopped completely. They were stumped when it came to explaining what was going on. They were completely stymied when it came to explaining why. And they sure as hell didn't stand a celluloid cat in hell's chance of agreeing between themselves what they should tell an expectant world. How could they explain the fact that the woman's skin showed no signs of weather even though she'd been found in scorching sun? In fact her skin was as pale as ivory. Despite the lashing sun and salty seawind.

There are stories pertaining to human babies who get raised by monkeys in the jungle – think of Mowgli, for instance, or Tarzan. And there are stories of primitive men enshrouded by snow flurries in the Alps or Himalayas. There is also a story about a woman in a boat which explains how the Basque language came to be. It's an oddity, that language. Not like other Indo-European tongues. So you'd need a myth to explain that.

To flee the sack of Troy, some of its wiliest and luckiest inhabitants fled in boats across the Mediterranean and rowed with all determination. But that wasn't enough to make the fugitives feel sufficiently safe. Many of the craft were deliberately sunk, leaving one and one only to beach at the wide mouth the Guadalquivir, in a marshy archipelago full of birds that seemed to be present on the wrong continent, such as glossy ibis and pratincoles. But even here the Trojan refugees felt nervous, so they separated.

One determined woman began walking inland. The long tracts of marsh, pierced by the weird cries of skulking birds

119

deep in the reeds, gave way to crumbled earth and tilled fields. Then, when her feet were blistered and raw from walking, she found herself trudging towards hills and then, finally, into the mountainous heart of Spain. Her feet bled as she traversed this rocky terrain but something drove her on.

Even on this high ground, amid this seeming emptiness, she would look behind her, convinced of pursuers. She imagined determined soldiers hell-bent on her destruction, carrying swords sharpened for her throat only. So on she went, on and on, until she arrived at mountains that were altogether higher. And so, in the Pyrenees, she learned to climb, to stretch her body and spirit in order that she might reach the isolated spot where she felt so remote from the world of human activity that she could breathe easily. She had a strategic vantage point to survey all that happened in the valleys below, where the rivers were tiny silver threads. Here, in this thin air, she decided to lose her language, to kill it as if with a stone, so that she could never be identified.

Months later she met a shepherd, and she spoke to him in a newly-minted language that only she knew, because she had invented it during her lonely sojourn in a land so high that only the Alpine choughs kept her company, cawing on the thin hint of thermals. It was a language born of paranoia, from the fear of pursuit, even here in this place of echoes. But it sounded right for these jagged peaks – harsh, clipped, the sound of tumbling scree and soughing wind.

She stayed with the shepherd and they took up residence in a hut which had little comfort. They used two stones for pillows, and challenged the cold by burning brushwood which took days to gather. Two years later they had the first of two children and by this time her made-up language was the language of all their lives. It was quite unlike any other, so each of them could add sounds or words as they saw fit. The skulking wolf had a name. The small white flower that clung on to the very tiniest of ledges was baptised by them. The white hare took its place in an evolving nomenclature of nature. They would happily exchange their new words in the evening, bringing the world into being by naming its parts. And in this way the Basque language came into being, spontaneous and fearful, the product of another special boat lady. *Ilargi. Ogi. Txori. Maite.* Moon. Bread. Bird. Love.

In another place, in another time, the other boat lady is making quite a stir, getting everyone in a flap.

No one had seen anything quite like this before. The experts got themselves in a lather. There she was, alive and dead at one and the same time. She breathed, yes, they recorded one breath, shallow and imperceptible other than with the sophistication of their machines. This suggested that she had to be sending some oxygen through her circulation, and yet that didn't seem to be the case. Her heart didn't beat. Her lungs were flaccid balloons. If you made the tiniest incision in her skin there was no blood. There was no pulse either. She was mystifying. There was the slow but certain rise and fall of her ribcage. Every day or so. One breath, in and out, as if the body was forcing itself to remember the essential rhythm. But little else. It was as if she was going through the motions.

When the distinguished cardiologist Matt Boran looked at what the phalanx of machines was telling him – the flatlining LCDs, the constant blips that were without neither peak nor trough – he felt as if he were about to undermine everything he'd ever been taught through his Harvard years and all the practical experience he'd gained in surgical theatres, working with the best. This woman cocked a snook at everything the Greeks knew, or intimated. It undermined medicine itself, and seemed to threaten all that was understood about life. Over the centuries the body had yielded its secrets, and people had been healed because of this. Anatomists had harvested facts alongside organs. Reason, brought to bear on the brain, had shown it to be a limitless machine, powered by electricity which ran across the synapses. Science had dissected the human frame and shown a design which was intricate and fascinatingly complete. But now this. This unhinging moment.

As he scrutinized his colleagues' faces for clues as to what they were surmising, Boran thought back to the experiments they'd done on dogfish in the laboratory. They had tried to chart the effects of taking away the heart and replacing it with an artificial pump. He'd felt then like some small God, even as he tried to justify his actions by saying that the creature didn't feel pain as we did. Without a heartbeat to supply a core beat, the fish couldn't time the rhythm of its swimming (and the effect of the major operation to remove the heart would have to be taken into account as well) and so, ridiculously out of synch, the fish thrashed around in the water, its normal sleek actions now spastic. And this extraordinary woman's heart didn't seem to beat, yet the lungs drew in air with a rhythm that had to be established by something. She drew a full breath every three days. Something determined that, drove the impulse. What on earth was it? And what happened to the oxygen she drew in?

As he stood there, as dumbfounded as the other distinguished visitors, watching the nothing-happening-here-move-right-along spectator show of the old woman on her bed, and at the ranks of mute sentinel machines, one of them started to spew forth numbers on graph paper, like ticker tape. Matt looked at them without the least inkling of what it all meant . . .

4557759990003428190 . . . 4557759990003428190 . . . 4557759990003428190 . . . 4557759990003428190 . . . 4557759990003428190

Over and over again the figures were repeated.

Boran wrote the numbers down. He was in the sort of daze in which a medic who's beginning to believe in miracles finds himself after too many hours looking at an old woman's unmoving face. He walked down to the canteen where he was due to meet a journalist from *People* magazine who was desperate for an exclusive. Boran had been deputized by the others to talk to him after the debacle following the press briefing by the man from the hospital, who had said one wrong thing which had found its way around the world in Chinese whispers, growing more and more preposterous with every news item. He knew he had nothing new to say, at least with any certainty. It all sounded too much like something out of *The X-Files*.

But everyone wanted to know stuff – medically, scientifically and commercially. Even the least detail, the most trivial tittle-tattle could be worth something. *Hello!* magazine could treble its circulation if the term 'world exclusive' could be bolstered by so much as a single fact. So Boran took a gamble. He gave the man the sequence of numbers, asked if his readers might be able to decode it. He felt as if they had nothing to lose.

Managing the media feeding frenzy could have kept an enormous number of people busy. There were thousands of people working on the story, with hundreds of journalists in or heading for Buenos Aires, the source of the newspapers. Kent Lachan was one of them, settling in for the long haul, working sixteen hours a day to find out where the paper boat came from.

The more the story grew, spread and took root, the greater the number of experts who flew in to Morris Hill. One afternoon there were no fewer than four Nobel Prize winners gathered around the bed, along with a number of medical pioneers and world authorities. All there to see Mrs Miracle, the Woman-Who-Sleeps.

Now here's a thing. Someone had to declare her dead so that she could be buried or otherwise disposed of. But as no one was willing to do that, to make that crucial call, she had to stay as she was. Thanatologists, who study death, have often debated the exact moment of death, but knowing when to switch off the machine was not in their ken. So you had a hospital under siege owing to the multitudes who wanted to see her. Some thought they could be healed through visiting her, and there were so many sick people and so many wheelchairs that you could have confused it with Lourdes, were it not for the serried ranks of the National Guard who guarded the hospital perimeter, with orders to shoot to kill, which even the State Governor thought too damned OTT. As if the wheelchair army was going to storm the building. Up the one ramp.

In Iowa a sinister cult had formed. It worshipped the lady from afar and had baptized her Marina, the woman of the sea. They had raised a temple to her, creating an outsize version of the paper boat out of reams and reams of newspaper, as they'd bought the entire back catalogue, every single issue of the *Iowa Herald*, going back to the late 1880s. These carried news of matters agricultural in the main. After all this was Iowa.

You could therefore read the boat in the spanking new temple as one long commercial for farmers, and see the history of tractors and the gorgeousness of local names. The latest model for the newest arrivals . . . the Avery 5-10 HP which does in an hour the work of a horse in a day – a bargain at $550. The Advance-Rumely Oil Pull. The Martini Caterpillar. The Monarch Neverslip. The Howard Steel Mule. The Cletrac Tank-Type, the kerosene burning Aultman-Taylor 15-30, the Profit Power Wizard that works magic on steep sides, the Nilson, the Waterloo Boy, the Lauson Full Jewel and, king of all it surveys, the Samson Sieve Grip, with an engine that will not stop.

One day she will come, they told themselves, dancing through the waving fields of wheat. Come to Iowa. That was the prophecy of One-Eye Sam as he read some bones in the remains of a fire, determining meaning in the fire-bleached fragments. And she would climb on board a Samson Sieve Grip, or at least an idol of her would be placed on the high seat, and she would arrive at a town such as Sac City or Sloan, and the cult members, driven wild by the sight of her, would strew wheat sheaves in front of her, much as they scattered palm fronds in front of Jesus on his donkey. And they would welcome her and assure her they would follow her anywhere, this dumb idol on a rusted tractor. They could set up an utopian community on the edge of a lake somewhere, live there forever, with her. Every single Marinero and Marinera had vowed to do anything for her, because she was the answer. They would give up their earthly goods to the next needy person, or crawl on bloodied knees along rocky paths until they trailed ribbons of torn flesh. They would even sacrifice their children Aztec style, or do it in the Jonestown manner, giving their offspring fizzy drinks laced with cyanide. And One-Eye Sam could see all of this coming. The incipient madness that will have them in its grip. He has seen spectral figures promising things, ghostly figures genuflecting somewhere in a future land. Never to each other. Just to Her. And his bloodshot eyes always know the curve of the future. Or his bloodshot eye, rather.

But Iowa was just the microcosm. The entire world had grown obsessed by Marina. Journalists – even the ones with integrity who worked for the last of the papers of record, those august organs – resorted to out-and-out fantasy, to making things up in the absence of hard facts or precious detail. The papers were like novelettes. The roster of experts on CNN and Fox was displaced by soothsayers and astrologers and self-styled prophets, not to mention the authors of the many books that had been turned round in a hurry, including a sumptuous coffee-table book with pictures of her taken from all angles, by a man who had photographed every royal family on this globe. Pictures bought for outrageous prices from surgeons with hidden lenses in their lapels. Television, like nature, abhors a vacuum, and the prattling zoo of seers, pathological liars and 'guardians of Marina's truth' filled the TV screen with bright, empty chatter, like a cage of hyperactive marmosets vying for space.

Ninety books will be written about the Woman-Who-Sleeps over the next decade, and no fewer than forty doctoral theses, not to mention the plethora of academic papers that keep teams of scholars in work from Uppsala to Missoula. The unnamed woman will grow to be the world's greatest celebrity, and everyone will have at least one personal story about her. For as the months pass, there won't be the least sign that the obsession is paling in any way. In Japan and America new TV channels will be created expressly to satisfy the need for material about her. Some will just beam out the same image of her day and night, like the burning Yule log that's broadcast in the run-up to Christmas and is watched by people in bars from Florida to the Canadian border. Some of the Japanese radio stations that used to broadcast ambient sounds – such as airport hubbub and rail station busyness, so that guilty men in hotel rooms could ring their wives and make up plausible excuses – *I'm afraid I've just missed the 17.42 or the 19.27 or even the last train home* – will start to broadcast Marina songs, the new hymns written to celebrate the dazzle of her existence.

When the burghers of Oakland decided to take her out of the hospital and place her back in the boat and put them both on display, it engendered the biggest and most animated global conversation ever. Shouldn't this have been a presidential decision? Or one for the UN? Google's servers crashed: that's how busy things got, with the internet hyperventilating with opinion, counter-opinion, hot-headedness, public outcry and public concern. It was as if there was a moral earthquake turning up the earth, cracking its crust. The Oakland Decision, as it was known, commanded the newspapers' front pages for a fortnight, a phenomenon unheard of, but despite events in Iraq and Afghanistan, the ongoing meltdown of banking and its reputation, with the rupture of house prices, the slide of Japan's economy, the glacial melt of the Dow Jones and the NASDAQ which left dozens of beleaguered CEOs dangling from home-made nooses; despite all this it was Marina who filled the news, who was the news. The *LA Times*, *Jerusalem Post*, *Straits Times*, the *Washington Post*, *Al Watan* in Damascus, the *Moscow Star*, all adorned their front pages with pictures of her.

She commandeers the news-stands of Argentina, of course. But the two men who could explain things and tell all, or at least say who she was, have died within a week of each other.

The doctor was mulched in a traffic accident on the road

128

to the airport by an enormous cross-country land-train, carrying a gargantuan cargo of Malbec from Mendoza. Horacio died because his heart was riven in two by grief after losing his soulmate. The only person who remains to tell the tale is Jaime, the boy from the upstairs flat, but as no one asks him, he tells no one. He realizes that he has something the world desires and even occasionally contemplates the financial worth, the monetary advantage of this sort of knowledge. Jaime has her name, knew the two of them, the dancing husband and wife, and can talk about her last journey in the boat. Built from materials he supplied, no less. But he keeps mum. He has his own stuff to deal with, anyway. Manuelito is now an unbidden constant in his life. But the two, Jaime and Manuelito, are no longer hostile to one another. One Tuesday, after a grand asado, the young man decides to confide all the details of the boat to Manuelito, who is dumbstruck by the tale of the river burial but appreciative of this act of disclosure, how it slings a bridge across a river, bringing them close.

When David first proposed it to Elsbetha she reacted in a typically incendiary manner. 'Why on God's earth would I want to meet this girl, David? She's your problem and you get paid to deal with her. Why should I get embroiled in your work, be sullied by all the harm that sloshes around? I'm trying to protect myself, can't you see that, you idiot? You absolute idiot.'

But she did thaw and David, Tierra and Elsbetha did go to the zoo together, by car to the Oakland ferry, thence by

BART and then the MUNI. When they arrived the little girl was entranced by the big breakers coming in off the sea beyond Highway 1. In the zoo she saw her first giraffe and her first peacock and, well, pretty much every animal for the first time.

Elsbetha had prepared a picnic, which they ate on the edge of the giraffe enclosure. Tierra was still hungry after they'd finished it, so they went to the café and shared a gargantuan pizza. As they sat there, Tierra was grateful and courteous and asked questions about animals in the same way that a girl called Betty once did in a story she'd heard. Elsbetha found herself drawn to the little girl, liked the eager timbre of her voice, and genuinely enjoyed her company. In the car on the way home, after dropping Tierra off at what Elsbetha took to be a less than desirable address, Elsbetha asked David if there was anything wrong with inviting her over to visit them sometime? As she asked the question her hand rested on David's shoulder and she didn't remove it, letting it settle there, as an act of trust.

Welcome to the offices of Specky Kravitz, a man without moral fibre. His office is just a desk, really, and it stands by itself in the middle of a large lock-up halfway between San Francisco and Sacramento, in an area which is full of redundant farm machinery and skulking crack manufacturers, and people like Specky, who live as far away as possible from the law.

The sun is a clementine suspended above the drained delta, generating a thin orange light suffused through fog.

130

It is sufficient to penetrate the gloom of Specky's place, where an electric treadmill is working overtime as a Rottweiler as big as most professional wrestlers runs its daily ten miles, dragging its enormous neck chain and still managing to average 1.6 miles per hour. Specky, formerly of the CIA, uses dogs a lot in his line of work, which varies a great deal, but is hardly ever conducted without threats and violent overtures. He learned some handy skills in El Salvador, techniques for maximizing pain, tricks to suit a man's worst tendencies.

On a chair in front of him sits Mr Pink, who's been out of Angola Prison over in Louisiana for eight months (which is a personal record), and next to him sits Mr Black. On the floor between them is a sack, and inside something is wriggling fit to burst.

'What's in the sack, gentlemen?'

'Not what, but who?' suggests Mr Black, who is wearing a retro zoot suit.

'Who then? Who is the struggling who? He's not a big one. A child?'

'A dwarf.'

'Don't get many of those nowadays. Must be something to do with screening. Life is a conundrum. What makes you think I want a dwarf? Do I look like the sort of criminal mastermind who'd feel the need to run himself a circus?'

'The dwarf's father. He would want him back. Of that we can be certain. So it's a prize. A prize dwarf.'

Mr Pink is smiling as he pokes the sack with a length of sharpened stick. There is a bleating sound; it sounds like a young goat stranded on a mountain ledge of terror. Mr Black picks up the story. 'We were down in some cantina, awash with margaritas, when one of us struck up with the question, who is the best person to kidnap in the city to get the biggest ransom? We dismissed obvious candidates as being too hard to get to, anyone with layers of security. We thought about this oil widow who lives all alone in Pacific Heights, but then she doesn't have anyone who cares enough about her to stump up. Then Spade Brewer suggested a hit on the McLarty family, not only because Larry McLarty is one of the richest people on the West Coast, but he also has the sort of personal protection that goes with it.'

'Forgive my intruding but didn't you say you wanted to avoid security? I thought you wanted to avoid lame ducks?'

'My cousin is part of that security team. And we also traded information about McLarty's brother-in-law, who works in the circus down near Pier One. He'd be easy to spot as he has a raspberry-coloured birthmark covering one half of his face. Apart from the port wine stain he is a dwarf. Easily identifiable, you might say.'

'Indubitably.'

That's how they'd ended up going to the circus the previous evening, brazenly taking up the best seats in among the disinterested rich kids who sat silently through it all, finding it more amusing to scrutinize the men in black, that is until one of them flashed a blade in their direction and drew the bead of a finger across his throat by way of silent warning. The men on a mission laughed at the clowning and were genuinely impressed by the Russian

132

trapeze artists who worked without a safety net and could have a fine career option in burglary should they choose. The man with his head in the lion's mouth, on the other hand, was stupid and a con. Everyone could see that the animal was so old his teeth had fallen out.

The dwarf didn't appear until the second act, when they were still eating their ice creams. He was driving a car which exploded every now and then so that the doors blew off, and the engine, which made a pathetic set of farting sounds, stopped dead in its tracks.

In the sack the dwarf made some strangled moans.

Before the show was over Mr White walked around to the back of the big top. When the dwarf returned to his make-up room Mr White was waiting for him with a wad of chloroform in his hand. Mr Pink then slunk in to help lift the sack.

Unbeknown to Mr White, a detective employed to ensure the safety of each and every member of the gangster's extended family had fitted a microtransmitter under the skin on the dwarf's wrist. When necessary he could pick them up on GPS, down to a pinpoint. Should he need to home in on one of them, the satellite could track them to within a breath, locate the microchip hidden under the dermis.

But, for now, before the Russian trapeze artist sounds the alarm, there's a vertically challenged captive thrashing about like a ferret in the sack. Specky turns off the treadmill and the rottie totters on jellified legs towards a porcelain plate, where a pile of Aberdeen Angus rib-eyes fit to sate the ravenous appetites of a tribe of lions awaits his devouring jaws.

Specky tells the two to phone McLarty PDQ and make sure they use a street phone as the fucker's always on a wiretap from some inquisitive outfit or other – narcs, Feds, IRS ne'er-do-wells. He suggests they request a direct transfer into a Cayman Island account he happens to know: gone are the days when black bags full of greenbacks are left under bridges in agreed locations. Specky writes down a series of numbers and passwords on a piece of thick parchment and uses a blotter to dry the ink. Not often you see a blotter nowadays. But Specky is a sophisticate, able to build impregnable walls around money, firewalls more secure than the Pentagon, oh, how much more secure than their ricepaper defences! There are FBI agents who can't sleep for thinking how to nail Specky's hide, but his hide is his own and will never be hung out on a fence to dry.

'And where are the others?' Specky asks as he fixes them gimlets to drink. He is partial to old school cocktails: not for him the Bacardi-based nonsense.

'They've gone to steal the paper boat.'

'*The* boat?'

'The very one.'

From the strangulated hessian of the sack the three men hear a plaintive voice, a guttural squeal.

'Please let me out. I need the john and I'm starving and you need me to be alive for your plan to work.'

'Not necessarily,' says Specky as he raises an assenting eyebrow. Mr White takes a knife to the knot in the neck of the sack. An unnaturally shaped head, sporting the unmistakeable port wine stain, comes into view, eyes blinking wildly as they adjust to the light.

Specky suggests they should sort things out over dinner, asking the dwarf what sort of toppings he'd like on his pizza. The newly released captive stutters an automatic list – jalapeños, pepperoni, double pineapple, black olives and plenty of anchovy. The man at Pizza Hawaii assures Specky he can get a delivery over in twenty minutes and Specky says that'll save him having to track down the pizza man's family and kill them. The menace in his voice is that of a camp guard knocking nails into his club.

The dwarf is out of the sack and standing on uncertain legs, or half-legs. The thought of pepperoni has made him salivate like a rabid leper. He is escorted to the can where he finds it hard to urinate even though his bladder is the size of a regulation football.

Meanwhile, the rest of the gang was living a parody of the opening scenes of *Reservoir Dogs*, sitting in a diner and in the full throes of a febrile discussion of Jennifer Lopez as an icon. There was even a dispute about the tip they should leave their cute Armenian waitress. Mr Scarlet said he never gave tips on principle, but the others weighed in with arguments culled from the film which they pressed on him with all the meanness their rattlesnake eyes could convey.

Unlike Tarantino's imagined gang, this one had lots of members and therefore more colours. Indeed some of them argued there were too many colours and so some of them are named after uncool hues. Mr Tangerine. Mr Magenta. Unlike their counterparts in the film this gang's working in linear time, so they all traipse out to the three cars in the lot knowing that if everything turns to shit in this gig no flashback's gonna save them. They are off to steal a paper boat.

They have a customer waiting in Brussels who has offered four million euros for it. Some of them feel so confident that this job will be carried out, will cruise to an easy success, that they are already daydreaming about what to do with their share of the money. One is skiing down the slopes of La Joya near Esquel, working up a thirst for his mistress in the Andean cabin where she lies, her thighs warming a polar bear skin as he slaloms his way down to her.

The client's go-between has fixed a rendezvous for the following night. Cash drop. No questions asked.

Even though Mr Pink has been to see the boat three times, and had to stay in line for five hours on both occasions, noting camera locations, the depth of steel around the plinth on which the boat rests and so on and so forth, the gang paid precious little attention to these details. There was a consensus favouring a simpler technique. Crash and bang. Haul ass double quick. Use a fuck-off truck to break in. A Mac 3000 Head Loader if they can steal one in time.

Light was seeping in from a widening sky. The streets empty of people. Mr Blue revved the engine of the juggernaut and it spewed a blue cloud of diesel fumes. The revs increased by the thousand as his foot pressed down.

He felt the power in the heavy vibrations, they turned him into a small God. He was on a hill overlooking the museum, the cab positioned like a prow, waiting for the phone message that would kick things off. Party time. The word now flashed up, not that Mr Cerulean intended to send it at that moment. He was just trigger-happy.

Mr Blue had gunned the engine to maximum throttle, and by the time he powered down Masonic the lorry engine was similar to an enormous scrub jay, angry and insistent, chack, chack, chacking. He took the corner savagely, with four wheels lifting despite the tonnage of bricks on board. He was almost at the gates when all the warning signs came pulsing through his neurones. Rather than a solitary nightwatchman, as Mr Pink had promised, he saw disciplined ranks of National Guard, lifting their automatic weapons as one. He didn't have time to warn anyone, or to veer away from the devastating volley of bullets that turned him into a bloody pulp as metal punctured and windows smithereened.

For the first time in their working lives the rest of the gang turned up punctually and were instantly involved in a shoot-out in the style of *Dodge City* where they were, of course, ill-matched against half the infantrymen of Camp Pendleton, especially when someone trained a powerful howitzer on the lead car, blasted out some very heavy ordnance and turned it into metal shards. It's possible that before the subsequent hail of ammo was unleashed someone shouted 'Stop' but that's up for debate. When Army investigators counted the spent rounds they collected almost two thousand without even looking in the drains.

The lorry did smash down the front walls of the museum and there was a heart-stopping moment when the soldiers thought it might careen all the way to the paper boat, but luckily it crashed to its final resting place near the Egyptian displays, which were themselves unharmed, guarded as they were by a legion of desert deities.

In that dawn light, among the whorls of dust, the boat seemed luminescent, the clouds of cordite like sea mist lapping around the base of the pedestal. A Ming vase, dislodged by the crash, rocked gently back into place. The dust settled.

In *Reservoir Dogs* the gang members die one by one. But life is unlike the movies, unless you're a spy in real life, or a superhero. So it was *Kansas City* or *The Untouchables,* rather going to the '*Dogs.* All those bullets. Zinging through the air like steel wasps.

Six months later, a mile from where her brother was assassinated, Tierra Doon was baptised in Mount Calvary Missionary Baptist Church, her body clad in a starched white gown as she was immersed in a marble pool, her soul cleansed and her sins absolved: a two-for-one deal. A coruscating light danced around her tiny frame.

Standing next to her was her mother, whose smile lit up the place. Behind her stood David and Elsbetha, who were now the girl's financial guardians. Tierra's mother was happy with the arrangement, which cushioned them from the cold economic winds that threatened to throw their world off its axis. David and Elsbetha have established a trust fund to pay for Tierra's education. She spends time with them, but only as much as she wants: there is no requirement. The deal is neither custodial nor legally binding. But Tierra enjoyed the things she did with them – such as the dancing lessons they took her to on Fridays. She had developed a taste for eating out and was no longer bashful about asking for her glass to be refreshed or sipping wine.

Tierra asked to be baptised in order to make absolutely certain she would go to heaven. There, she knows, Nu Nu is waiting for her, and she will take him some music, let him listen to what's new on the streets. He will play his guitar for her, and it will be the most comforting thing. She's certain he'll play some Stevie Wonder, knowing how it makes her smile. 'Isn't She Wonderful?' maybe.

There is a funeral taking place at the same time over on the Emeryville side of the city. Specky Kravitz and his dwarf accountant are in attendance: they get a mighty discount because they are forever sending people to their deaths, and gangland burials are always the fanciest. One man had diamond-encrusted handles on his coffin, which were jimmied off before they put him in the earth. Many members of the Oakland Police Department are there, secretly happy in their hearts to see so many bad guys killing other bad guys. It helps keep the streets safe, although innocents are sometimes caught in the crossfire, or struck by wayward bullets. The commissioner thinks it's a fine thing that so many should have gone to the Great Prison in the Sky in a little under three weeks. He keeps looking at his watch, as he has a meeting with the Mayor at three, and he knows the young buck doesn't share his enthusiasm for dead gangsters.

But the media hardly notices this funeral. Not today, when the President himself is opening the exhibition, the craziest, darnedest exhibition in the whole sprawling history of exhibitions. The strangest in the city's history, that's for sure. Despite the fact that the museum is still missing its facade, Ticketline has been under siege, with no fewer than eight million tickets sold already, and every hotel room in the city is booked up, and hordes of people are leaving to stay with relatives in Portland, San Antonio, anywhere really, so they can let out their homes to these, well, pilgrims. The Pope is coming to Oakland next spring. The Dalai Lama's already been. San Francisco is in the shade of the event, and even though it's only a crow-hop away tourists don't go there anymore. Oakland is blessed: it says so on the T-shirts.

This city of six hundred thousand souls is being totally changed, not least by the fact that each and every denizen gets a free ticket to go to see the lady resting. And they mix and mingle with the travellers from far away, who carry bawling children, outsize rucksacks, offerings to place at her feet. They come here to celebrate life and answer their questions about it, to understand what the fuss is all about, or just to buy some souvenirs. Most just want to look at the old woman for a little while, and become aggrieved when they are encouraged to move along – like the shovers and pushers at the Sistine Chapel who make the crowd flow. Some see her breathe. Others see her not breathing. Dormant. Almost dead. And when does death occur,

140

anyway? When the vital spark is finally extinguished? Or just before? Or when the ECG machines fail to register so much as a neural flicker? Some see her as an effigy. Others as a fountain of hope. *Take your pick, lady, but keep on moving, keep that line moving.*

The sleeping lady's power is that she is able to satisfy every expectation, fulfil every promise, answer all prayers. And all she has to do is lie there and let people project their hopes, their aims, their fears on to her wax parchment face and she absorbs some, reflects others, is an answering voice, a vessel for their fears, anything they want her to be, really. To someone who's just lost a grandmother to wild dementia she looks like a serene grandmother. To a visitor from Iowa, she looks like a goddess. And to someone from the right part of Buenos Aires she might look awfully familiar. But that's yet to happen. For now the shroud of secrecy is immaculate.

Chapter 4

Her Long Voyage

In New York, in Manhattan, amidst the retinal fizz of the eye-assaulting LCD messaging of Times Square, which included some enormous new adverts for a store actually called Mammon, there was celebration akin to the millennial New Year, with revellers popping champagne corks and some drinkers marooned on islands of sorrow, or maudlin with bourbon, or simply awash with sapping emotion. It's not every day a God comes through.

The revellers and spectators were all dealing, singularly and severally, with the fact that she was leaving these shores, and she would not be returning, not in their lifetimes, anyway. Some were cheered by the fact that she was taking her special brand of happiness and hope to the rest of the world. To tell them all that there are more things on heaven and earth than are dreamt of in their philosophies. That miracles can and do happen, just when you're least expecting them, and they don't have to be showy. They can be quiet – quietly extraordinary. That's what she told them, all that and more, without ever moving her lips. Yet despite her raging silence she impacted on people mightily. There were many who wanted to keep her among them. They felt churlishly selfish and wanted her to bless America for ever. Stay with them and let them be her boon companions.

Snaking through Harlem and out towards the opening vistas of leafy Central Park and then on to Broadway went her entourage, part funeral, part Rio carnival, a little bit showbiz, a liberal touch of reverence, a motorcade moving past the yelling crowds to the brownstones of Greenwich Village, which had been painted especially so that the place was a catalogue of modern paints – blue reflection, teal green, absolute white, bitter cherry, positive banana – with a soundtrack of marching bands, ululating faithfuls, short people craning their necks until complete but ursine strangers hoisted them on to their shoulders so they could get a glimpse as she passed. The police motorcycle lights made the streets look like a poor man's discothèque in the failing wintery light, dissipating blue streaks over the Hudson, wavelets tipped now by shimmery ripples of reflected neon.

There she goes, serene and implacable. Lift your grandchildren high, so they can mark this for their posterities. Tell their children, *I saw it with my very own eyes!* The Leaving.

She affected everyone. Her power was her serenity. She was a lake of stillness, like the glacial pooling of snowmelt in the lee of the col. Plate glass. Millpond. A chill area of standing water. But beneath its tranquil surface – unruffled by breeze, there was a great tonnage of water, in this rocky scoop. It could devour the valley below, raze its very memory from the surface of the land, should it be released, see its aqueous potential realized. In half an hour, maybe. Wouldn't take more than that. And that's the sort of power she has. Lakelike. Untapped. Unrealized. But there, impossibly there. Along with her secrets.

Representation from the entire United Nations was arrayed on the quayside near the midtown terminal and arrayed all the way to the Port Authority building, with many in full national dress and the others dressed in formal evening wear, as if this was one of those events where elegant creatures flit from table to table in chandelier-lit halls. Military bands were there to serenade her, along with underground hip hop artistes who had lugged their sound systems over from Brooklyn and played out of the back of vans. To add to the cacophonous mix there were samba dancers and salsa orchestras, voodoo men with loads of brass, Rastafarians with bass speakers to set the world atremble, school pipe bands, all playing with gusto and abandonment: to see Her on Her way.

She was carried in a bulletproof case adorned with the finest filigree of gold – a gift from a spanking new church in Tegucigalpa in Honduras. It was placed on a magnificent platform carved from a single trunk of Lebanon cedar by a blind school in Minnesota whose pupils had created bestiaries and phantasmagorias. They had whittled complete phyla of deep-sea creatures, as if blindness was a special kind of bathyscaphe which allowed you to travel down into the dark murk to spot wonders. A ghost dolphin broke for the surface through a fractured marquetry of pieces of French alder. A shoaling busyness of tropical fish patterned out across softwood sides and played hide-and-seek in swirling coral made of beech and birch.

She was beautiful there, on her elegant dais. The fact

that the strips of newspaper that made up the boat had yellowed made her face whiter, seemingly carved out of alabaster, verging on whitewash, absolute white. The woman who wasn't alive but who breathed once in a rare while. As odd as it gets.

To keep the crowd in order NYPD had allocated almost all of its force, leaving just a rump for essential duties, and they beetled into position along intersections, and stood three deep. The nearer you got to the ship the more the streets were filled.

The ship was the transatlantic liner, the *Queen Elizabeth II*, adapted for her new purpose and filled to the brim with treasures of all kinds. Its name had been changed in a ceremony drenched in Moët & Chandon, in which the spewing of ticker tape was matched only by the waterfalls of bubbly. The throne room of the ship, *Marine Star*, had been converted into a ceremonial viewing room for the Woman-Who-Sleeps.

The British Royal Family had grudgingly given their consent. Now that they were confined to their only palace at Balmoral, and Republican anger at their profligacy and arrogance had resulted in them losing their salaries from the public purse, the changing of the name of the ship was just the latest insult. For as a new religion built up around the woman, taking root in the United Kingdom as in so many countries, the King saw his role as Head of the Church dwindle and diminish, and eventually he had to abdicate his throne. The Royal Family could afford to employ only a handful of servants, but as one acerbic commentator suggested in a newspaper column, surely the

King could learn to wipe his own arse? Truth be told, the whole family had been given an option, namely to take up land in the Australian outback, gifted by their former subjects Down Under, who would be happy to find out how they'd cope with brown snakes and exploding eucalypts. They hated that Royal arrogance more than the Poms did.

Because they had had to install the best security possible – the ship had to be target *numero uno* on any global terrorist's shopping list – it had taken a while to get the ship ready, but once they realized that, what with the naval backup and the sky cover they had created one of the safest places on earth, they decided to fill the ship with other artefacts and treasures, so that people queuing to see Marina would be able to enjoy other wonders.

Before she left New York there had been a 24/7 line which more than matched the funeral queues of Lenin, Lennon, Mao and Diana all rolled into one. It also signalled that they weren't worried about terror. After all, she had her own battalion of soldiers devoted to her – a gift from the US which could ill afford to give up so many battle-hardened men, what with the ill-judged wars they were still prosecuting. They were the Pink Berets, like the Green Berets, except their caps were pink to denote the fact that they were all gay. Because of the innate homophobia of the Army, they had an inner steel tempered by exposure to hostility and hatred. Their unofficial slogan was *Harder than the Marines*, and they liked to play up to their reputation as often as they could. Hard men. Afraid of absolutely nothing. They would fuck with the Foreign

Legion. Literally. That's what they said. These are the only soldiers who paint their toenails. Any colour they like. Teal green, if they want to. Or robin's egg, that's in fashion.

They guarded her and her alone: the other treasures were left to other people, lesser soldiers. There was an array of incredible African jewellery airlifted from a Texan trillionaire's home in Houston which attracted considerable opprobrium: that a family could have kept such value and interest away from the public gaze for so many years! Some of the stuff had never been catalogued.

Egypt contributed a priceless collection of antiquities from the Valley of the Kings, which had been stolen by gravediggers years ago. These were revealed to an outraged storm of academic interest as they had only just been recovered after an enormous cross-border police operation. Relics from two thousand years before the birth of Christ. Stolen from beneath the sand.

So the old – as old as Chephren, Cheops and Mycerinus – travels with the new. And huge audiences all over the world view the hieroglyphs of nature, the stone represent-ations of reed beds and food items for consumption in the afterlife which travel with Flavia, who may or may not be in an afterlife all of her own. The oasis dwellers so wanted to ensure eternity. She had it thrust upon her.

So when she docks in her next destination the visitors in their impossible hordes will pass the innards of Ramses, file past rare scarabs and marble skulls representing the cow goddess Hathor and the hippopotamus river goddess Tawaret, then admire ranks of gold sarcophagi. On past

Ramses II, that original colossus, and then snake past the brown petrified bodies of mummies, wrapped like babies, and the visitors will often dwell on their own mortalities, as you have to when you're seeing such mad preservation. The tiny toenails bring on tears, not to mention the frozen look on faces that are just about to embark on a journey to the world of bulrushes and ample grapes. But why all this talk of Egypt when Marina should be the focus of all? Some believe she is Ramses' wife. There was a prophecy that she would arrive on a shore in a boat of papyrus. It figures. And that would explain the smirking grin on the colossus' face. That he is happy to see her.

So maybe she is an old lady from Buenos Aires who was actually a goddess. Maybe her life cycle goes like this, following the Egyptian pattern: *Ka*, the soul, is made on a giant wheel by the potter Khnum the instant you come into the life. Then *ba*, the spirit often signified as a bird, usually a stork, then the heart and then the shadow. At the gateway to the afterworld the heart would be weighed on scales with just a feather as counterbalance, the singular feather of truth and justice. If it overbalanced then the heart would be swallowed by an animal half crocodile and half hippopotamus. May your feather be light when you go on the great voyage to the afterlife, traveller.

In the *Marine Star*, beyond the Egyptian extraordinariness, there are racks of tropical birds' eggs in mahogany cases, gathered by an obsessive collector from Belize. On deck ten, the Deck of Books, you can view the *Big Book of Marina*, along with a library of other astonishing tomes:

books from Caxton's pioneering press, intricate manuscripts from medieval scribes and a Gutenberg Bible, still able to astonish with the meticulous craft and care with which it was produced. Books bound for Rio and New Orleans, where patient people will file past, taking in some of the detail.

This vessel is going to all points, to harbours busy as beehives, from Hong Kong with its rickety regatta of sampans, to Shanghai with its flashes of financial muscle and mushrooming towers of plexiglass, the skyscrapers that stretch upwards and ever upwards. She will visit Taiwan and its problematic Chinese mirror image in Chaozhou on mainland China. On she'll go, taking in Bremen's heavy industry, flirting with the glitterati of Monaco, testing the humidity of Carolina, skirting the dazzling lagoons of Venice, finding safe harbour next to the castellated wine storehouses of Varna in Bulgaria, sailing past the romantic architecture of Montreal, avoiding the mud sludge of the Mersey as Liverpool celebrates her with a Beatles reunion, being among merchants in Rotterdam, letting Antigua dance, cutting through iced channels and paralyzing cold in the approaches to Stockholm and the fey delights of Copenhagen. In every port the people throng. Hundreds. Thousands. Tens of thousands.

In Bremen they estimated that half the population turned out to greet her, an occasion marred by a tragedy which claimed the lives of twenty Turkish migrant workers who had built a makeshift platform on the flat roof of their apartment so their friends could gather for a bird's-eye view of the cortege. This then collapsed onto the street, onto the twenty-deep crowd arrayed on the pavement. For once the newspapers were right to invoke the word 'carnage'. The swiftly arranged collective funeral for the eighty-nine people who lost their lives, including nine children, was controversially combined with the welcoming ceremony for Marina, the terminality of their deaths made uncertain by the presence of someone who had in some ways defeated it. On television it attracted the biggest audience in history, which was ironic as this event was the harbinger of the end of television, as it was pretty much rivalled by the amateur journalists who streamed it live from their handhelds into their palmtops and then sent it out there on the internet.

No plane can use the airspace above the ship, and the foolish Somali pirates who came on a reconaissance trip didn't get within a hundred nautical miles before they were warned off, a warning they failed to heed and so ended up being turned into matchsticks by an Italian fighter squadron scrambled from Sicily. Every country with a coastline has donated at least one ship to accompany the liner on its travels, and Bolivia, despite its being utterly landlocked, has donated some sailors from the tiny navy of Titicaca. They are short sailors, used only to lake patrol, but they are proud to serve.

When the ship docks people tend to pause for a moment when they enter the Room of Ashes, just before they see the *Big Book*, which is in the penultimate room before Hers. The rank smell of burning upsets them as it stings the inner lining of the nostrils. Is the ship on fire? It has been arranged thus, with that fine librarian and exquisite reader Alberto Manguel winning the plaudits for suggesting the nature of the display, the piles of burned parchment and smoke-damaged books.

These are books that people have burned at one time or another, out of rage or outrage. Blackened spines and charred covers. Salman Rushdie's *Satanic Verses* smuggled out of Iran, an act more dangerous by far than smuggling them in. An outsize glass case is filled with copies of the Talmud, far and away the most popular book to burn in the whole savage history of humanity. They torched it in Lublin, Paris, Cairo and even, in one anomalous incident, in West Texas, in a Christian uprising which was stamped out before it really got going. And next to those are the latest volumes to get the heat treatment: *Harry Potter and the Sorceror's Stone*, set ablaze by the ever reliable Zippo lighters of some wacko fundamentalist evangelicals in Pennsylvania who wanted to burn J.K. Rowling at the stake. They saw this as twenty-first century witchcraft, and one of them, who went to see the film, dropped dead of a monumental heart attack as the boys at Hogwarts played a round of Quidditch. God is love. God is love.

So this is what the barely moving lines of pilgrims and sightseers see – the interface between the savage and the civilized. The barbarian armed with a box of household matches and a rag of petrol.

When the first copy of the book of faith devoted to Marina was publicly torched, by an outraged Sufi master who railed against what he saw as the essential heresy of the Woman-Who-Sleeps, the officials of the nascent church

151

made absolutely sure they got the ashes of the book back. The holy, holy ashes.

The centrepiece of the Room of Ashes is a small collection of books with primrose-coloured covers and a script, entirely unfamiliar to the majority of the spectators, that runs exotically across its front and spine. But this is a highlight. Why? Because rumour has it that these were her favourite books, although how you'd actually prove that when no one knows her identity even is an irony lost on the majority. Yet there is this common assertion, which conjures her up in a hermit's cell, on a lonely mountain, reading these pale yellow tomes. This yellow-covered quartet of novels. The Buru Quartet.

In some of the darkest, most septic times in the modern history of Indonesia, when a dictator ruled with an iron fist in a chain-mail glove, an author, Pramoedya Ananta Toer, lived to write. The man who ruled his native country was unspeakably cruel. His flagrant abuses of power, married to a rabid paranoia, created a country where brother would betray brother without a second thought, because they were afraid of their own thoughts, and would stifle them if they could, like suffocating babies with pillows. Pramoedya was arrested in 1965 and there and then every book he owned was burned, creating a bonfire of learning, a conflagration of criticism, high-licking flames of determined scholarship. Verbs exploded like firecrackers. Tenets fed the flames like toluene.

The policemen who arrested the bewildered author – he only wanted to write, what crime was that? – had eyes that betrayed no flicker of kindness. They had irises of ice, a glacial hatred burning beneath the stencilled eyebrows of men who might have been taken for cartoon policemen, had they not had blood on their hands, caked under fingernails, evidence of someone forced to squeal.

To understand that look in their eyes you'd best listen to this joke about Auschwitz, and before your liberal sentiments are too madly upset it might be at the very least placating to know that this one was told many times by the senior rabbi at the West London Synagogue. As it happens he donated the charred Talmuds also.

A Jew was caught stealing something of little intrinsic value in the camp, a potato maybe, which could feed ten, given the sort of hunger that consumed their souls in this devilish place, or maybe he had just torn out a page from a book. The Jew is dragged before the Commandant who says that the usual punishment for any crime in the camp is certain death, but he explains that today he is feeling lenient because he has just returned from Berlin, where the finest of their German scientists have made him a glass eye identical to the real one. He suggests giving the petrified Jew a sporting chance, saying that if he can tell which is which he might, he just might, spare his life. Without a moment's hesitation the Jew states that the right eye is the real one. When the Commandant asks him how he knew the Jew says that in the other there was just a hint of compassion.

The secret police have glass eyes through which they can only see a world of victims. They beat Pramoedya to within an inch of his life, and in so doing destroy his hearing, leaving him with a maddening hiss where once was music.

Of course there wasn't a judge or any hint of legal process, just a verdict based on little evidence. The author was taken before a general who was having his nails buffed by a woman in military fatigues. He never deigned to look at Pramoedya, although he did scold the woman for revealing too much cuticle on one of his middle fingers, before insouciantly telling the guards to take the prisoner away. And they took him a long way, to the island of Buru, where he languished for thirteen years, denied even the most basic rights, living in insanitary conditions, with nothing like sufficient nutrition. His skin became translucent, verging on transparent. He fattened crickets and grasshoppers on tiny piles of coconut dust so that the insects would taste of something edible when his teeth crunched on their hard carapaces.

One year he obtained a pencil from a sympathetic guard – there would be others during his time there but they were always mavericks, exceptions to the bile-hearted norm – and started to compose a work of fiction. When the graphite ran out he started to memorize each new sentence, every fluent turn of phrase and plot. They would eventually result in the Buru Quartet, the jaundice-coloured volumes that people stop to look at as their heartbeats begin to quicken as they realize they are almost within sight of Her.

No one knows how the rumour started circulating that these were her favourite books, and there is something wondrous about the selection. To imagine the old woman alive and reading the Indonesian version of *War and Peace* with its sugar farms and concubines, redacted by the author to as many of his fellow prisoners as would listen, so terrified was he that he would forget connecting plots, or that his entire memory of it would be expunged by the blow of a guard's heavy piece of bamboo. As luck – not that he was allowed such an optimistic word – would have it, he was allowed a typewriter in his latter years at Buru, and then he clacked away at the metal keys. He could see the fingers hitting the letters, noting how desperately they punched away. Sometimes he would imagine he was hearing the sound of a wave breaking and he would tell himself that it was the sound of a perfect sentence turning in on itself. In the silence he recorded the existence of all his stories, which had also been memorized by other prisoners just to be on the safe side, committed to memory by academics, serial rapists, murderers and thieves and, this being Indonesia in a dark and troubled time, a lot of innocent listeners, caged for no crime.

He was the last to leave Buru, a changed but infinitely wiser man, and on his release in 1979 he had to live under house arrest for a further thirteen years. But his masterpiece is on board the *Star* and a kindly monk from Bhutan is on hand both to read and translate parts of the book to anyone who is interested. Once he read it all aloud, every single sentence, and it took a year and a quarter to do so. He tried to learn it as he went, but his was the silence of forgetfulness, which is appropriate enough, as the most important thing about any novel is what is forgotten, or is presumed to have been forgotten.

As he read the quartet, the monk neglected matters such as eating, or visiting the latrine. He immersed himself in the words, dived into their depths, hunting for pearls,

155

amazed by the shimmer that reflected from the shoals of beautiful nouns. His presence was proof, as if more was needed, of the way in which many religions had come to an accommodation with the new faith, cult, religion, call it what you will. They have to, really. She is the personification of the *zeitgeist*, a woman for the New Millennium, despite her seeming catatonia. The mix of truths and specious nonsense seems to suit people: it animates them, makes them feel again.

There isn't time to visit all the rooms on board, with their treasures aplenty, but should you get a ticket do pop in to see former Archbishop Reilly, who is the custodian of the Bible room. He does a wonderfully animated talk about martyrs, in which he pretends to set himself ablaze, and at one point performs a magic trick in which he decapitates himself with an infidel sword, but it's really just a watermelon. It makes a terrifyingly lifelike and bloodily slurping sound as the blade slices through. Don't take the children. Once, going through the Panama Canal, Reilly got a bit flummoxed, cutting off part of his scalp. The bloodletting reminded some visitors of movies in the *Scream* series, with their ketchup amputations.

Those on board entrusted with safeguarding Marina didn't give two hoots about the dazzling array of treasures: they had one focus and one focus alone, and that was ensuring her safety. Any one of her guardians wouldn't hesitate to give up his life for her, without a nanosecond's hesitation. This was a human shield like no other: trained to kill and trained to die, bound for any port big enough to take the big liner. Some have dredged new approach channels, and some have created new harbours, as nobody wishes to miss out. Sydney. Galveston. Cadiz.

On her peregrination she attracts new worshippers as well as legions of the curious, who often join the converts. From continent to continent, in all directions. From the chill waters around Valparaíso to the soupy humidity of Veracruz, from Gdansk to Casablanca, through millpond waters and feisty weather, Trieste to Tunis, from the safe haven of Okinawa to a wintry Vladivostok, from ebullient Marseilles, round the Horn, on to crowded Cape Town, to whaling waters, past rocky pinnacles, Melbourne, Malaga, Azov, Tangi and Khoe. And one special visit, to a place few liners visit.

They dock offshore at Easter Island, as the carved heads have been so much a part of the world's bank of legends for such a long time, waiting patiently for her ship to cleave the thin charcoal line of the horizon. Patiently, silently, waiting for her appearance. So they lift her off the ship and let her grace the land of Easter Island. And someone swears that one of the heads moves as she does so, and so another part of the legend is born, just as the statuary drift off to sleep, their excitement over. And it does look as if they're sleeping, and it does look as if they resemble the old lady. A case of people projecting their desires onto the moai, or just echoing those of the people who first carved them, these weighty statues with their eyes of burning red coral?

On board the ship, the Polynesians, who paddle out in their surprisingly seaworthy canoes, are affected by Her in the same way as so many. They pay attention to the many treasures on board but she is incomparable. Are the facts the thing? The breathing without a circulation of the blood. The fact that she might live for ever, if this is living? Or is she a glimpse of the halfway world, the suffocating purgatory some get trapped in? Whatever. There she lies. Her skin uncannily translucent. Her eyes seemingly sentient and asleep. They listen to her breath, aghast. One unbelievable breath.

Marina! Marina! Marina! Marina! Their hearts sing with her name, do her breathing for her. In her hibernation, her no-woman's-land.

And if you stand awhile and look carefully, look clearly, you might glimpse yourself as a child, full of rampant hopefulness, before the world besieges you with hurt and pain. She is like you then, but without the germ of fear. She is as you would wish your life to have been. Beyond harm. Safe from spite. Content just to rest for as long as possible.

Flavia. Marina. The Woman-Who-Sleeps. The Goddess. She. The Innocent. In her bed in a titanic ship, within all the other chambers filled with exquisite memorabilia, so that she is a Russian doll, a puzzle more profound than any other. *Marina!*

She has been around the world three times already. But not to Buenos Aires. Which is remarkable, all things considered.

Kyle Lachan, ace reporter, is still ferreting around in Buenos Aires, sensing that he is coming to the end of his search. He sleeps in hotel rooms with mirrors in the ceilings, dreaming of finding a name, an address, an informant with some information.

And on she goes, along the great sea lanes, through squalls of gulls and squadrons of storm petrels, from harbour to harbour, from swelling crowd to hysteric convention. Just lying there. On and ever on.

Name. *Ka. Ba.* Heart. Shadow.

On and on.

The real action was under the surface, a biological phenomenon of migration and primal drive, marvellous as wildebeest traversing the Serengeti, or the titanic flutterings of monarch butterflies as they crossed continents. Even the most cynical marine biologist would have to reach for the lexicon of miracle to describe the wonders underwater. Myriad fish followed the ship as if it had the magneticism of the moon, emptying great swathes of water, leaving them bereft of fish.

As she approached Europe there were irridescences of herring of course, mixed with tunny and scad, wriggling pilchards and shimmers of anchovy. Lozenge-shaped shoals of fish such as smelt, which when they are caught smell of cucumber, wriggled their way ahead. There were Norway pout, blue whiting, lesser argentines and snake blennies all in purposeful mix. Larger fish flanked them, the corkwings, the rock cook, goldsinny and cuckoo wrasse. And there were ugly buggers too, such as bull routs – all spine and sharpness – not to mention the wolf fish, a frightening fish which normally loses its head before going on fishmongers' slabs lest customers be scared. These, naturally, came in packs, and might have snarled their anger at being drawn away from the warmer middle waters. Or maybe just mad about being born hideous, those prognathous jaws strong enough to crush armourplate crabs at a snap, that mouth that appears saddened by being so seemingly deformed.

All over the northern seas fishermen pulled up empty nets, took off their sou'westers and scratched their briny pates, discombobulated by the total lack of fish in purse seines and beam trawls. The North Sea seemed pretty much denuded as if all the auguries and warnings of conservationists and fishing police about one day fishing them dry had come invincibly true.

Underwater a veritable natural history pageant moved as a living shadow for the ship as she progressed, rokers and stingrays pulsed ahead, all flat muscle while wondrous species such as ribbonfish – eels by all appearances – snaked inevitably onwards.

And from the lightless depths, drawn up from reefs dark as anthracite, littered with the rusted and seawormed bones of shipwrecks, came fish so transparent they made jellyfish seems overly substantial, and angler fish, too, with tiny lanterns of phosphorescence hanging about devil's orb eyes.

From all the deepermost places and uncharted marine trenches, from Borkum Riff to Coral Bank, Silver Pit to Skagerak, the bottom feeders came blinking into the light, running the risk of blowing apart as they did so, as the pressure changed, but they had to come, despite the risk of explosion, pulled ever onwards and upwards by the invisible shape of a boat, fathoms above. Magnetising the shimmering shoals.

On and on. On and on, inexorably.

Chapter 5

Marina's Welsh Worshippers

In this country there are waterfalls that channel churning white water over Gothic overhangs, and they are in their way perfect. In Llanrhaeadr-ym-Mochnant there's one which is described as one of the Seven Wonders of Wales. It foams and tumbles in a way that would gladden a Romantic poet's surging heart. Wordsworth would have conniptions on seeing it, he really would. All that surge, all that primordial foam.

But there are also lurid flows of human vomit, down in the capital, where the native difficulty with alcohol is magnified, as if in a scientific demonstration. Look at the primitive failure to metabolize. The unsteady gait. Open-mouthed as the figure in Edvard Munch's *The Scream*, they hurl and chunder whatever they've eaten, or at least swallowed in the previous six hours. The undigested pastry and barely masticated bits of steak draw down the gulls, which hoover them up with avidity. Some of the roisterers are sick because of the amount of discount booze they've employed to drown their considerable sorrows, but others have foolishly ingested death kebabs, on Caroline Street, where the globules of polyunsaturated fat hang heavy in the air and you can order your meal with extra bacteria, without irony. *Streptococcus C, sir? Coming right up.*

Caroline Street. How does one explain the deeply central role of this five-hundred-yard rat-run of chip shops, Turkish takeaways, soft porn emporia and gay bars in the psyche of the city? Food so laden with cholesterol you can have a heart attack just reading the menu. And what exactly is in a Barry Island Softsteak Pie? I know a thousand people who've eaten them without necessarily having the foggiest. What lurks beneath the pastry, and what the fuck is that stuff resembling meat? Condemned meat, at that, after a quick run through the liquidizer. A fog-grey gloop that might be gravy – gravy as imagined by a Martian. What is it exactly? What manner of person buys this stuff? Have they lost all of their senses?

One afternoon a man called Tom Drinkall, who worked for Trading Standards in the city, happened to be walking down Caroline Street, on his way to deal with a complaint about dodgy digital cameras being sold in J & S Lenses, when he saw something move in Tony's 'world famous' chippy. The bloated rat, gnawing its way through a sausage in batter in the most leisurely manner, looked fit to burst, as full as a tick with the first sausage it had eaten. Slowly, like Sir David Attenborough creeping up on a gorilla in Rwanda, Tom reached for one of the deficient cameras. In one deft move, of which he was later enormously proud, he took a photo of the rodent as evidence. It happened that the camera worked perfectly, just this once. *Say cheese!*

This is a street that has seen a great many changes over the years, and not a little excitement. It used to host a good many late-night drinking clinics in the days when pubs shut early. Here you could enjoy a horse-meat steak washed down with that black wine from Eger, Bull's Blood. A wine to wrestle you to the ground and pummel the air out of your sides as if you were an old-school wrestler like Daddy Haystacks or as if Jackie Pallo has you in a vice-like grip, or a half nelson.

Halfway along Caroline there used to be a famous club called Bloomers but someone attacked it with a petrol bomb, burned it to the ground. In the *Echo* the day after the conflagration the stalwart cartoonist, Gren, had captured the moment in an exquisite image. Caroline Street with a gaping hole like a tooth extraction: above it, dwarfing all the buildings, is an atomic mushroom cloud and there are two men flying throught the air above the caption 'Now that's what I call a curry.'

The most popular dish on the street is chicken-curry-off-the-bone-with-chips, made from shredded meat from doomed hens which have never seen the light of day in their claustrophobic sheds and a sauce that manages to taste of nothing at all, despite its khaki colour. Khaki! The bars in the area, such as Green Cockatoo and Embrace are laboratories to test just how much cheap booze one needs to imbibe before losing all semblance of locomotive powers, to be unable to put one foot in front of another because you've forgotten where your feet are exactly.

Bacardi Breezer, Goldschläger Attack, Moscow Mule, Slow Comfortable Screw, Sex on the Beach: this is the litany of ferocious cocktails that paralyze and numb. Top of the list is vodka and Red Bull, one to knock you out and one to rev you up, coma versus combat duty. Little wonder, then, the drinkers are like guinea pigs, as if someone is observing, with clipboards and stopwatches noting how quickly tonight's exclusive offer, one strong lager and a double Sambuca for two quid – can lead to blastification. In Walkabout and Revolution the poor dabs are confused as if in a bomb blast, as if someone managed to perform a secret lobotomy on them somewhere between drink number seven and drink number eight. Not that they're counting. Not that some of them can still count. On the dance floor their arms flail like windmills. *Do ya think I'm sexy*, they mouth along to the music. Some produce more saliva than they would wish, their lips rimmed with foam. Sexy? Don't think so.

And listen, especially in the spring, to the essential sound of the Cardiff sky – the cries of the lesser black-backed gulls, which nest on pretty much every flat roof in the city. One tavern keeper on Clive Road had so many on the roof above the beer garden that the city's official naturalist was able to classify it as a colony. The finest medieval Welsh poet, Dafydd ap Gwilym, likened the gull to a nun, in pristine habit. In this city they line up on the flat roofs in incredible ranks and their nests are incredibly rank. Their cries are heartaches for herring, yearnings for delicious mackerel. They are everywhere, now that they can dine alfresco on the refuse dump and nest on chimneys.

And maybe, as we describe the city, we should mention the fact that this is where the Devil now lives, biding his time and waiting awhile, as he expects the visit of the Woman-Who-Sleeps. He's an opportunist trickster and he can see some advantage to his being here when the action happens, although he can't say exactly why. He used to sell

164

those new flats down Cardiff Bay, but business has come to a standstill so he's ducking and diving now, being the chancer that he is instinctively. He did fill his address book with the personal details of venal, greedy people, though, and that will come in handy, no doubt about that. They didn't want somewhere to live: they wanted a five-room money-making machine. But the bubble-maker burst.

He's been thinking, the Devil has: the people who've been to see the woman have probably carried some of her power away with them, not that he knows the precise nature or wellspring of it. So when she arrives in this tawdry capital she'll have dwindled, and that's when he'll pounce, or at least take something like affirmative action. Whatever that may be. Things used to be easier in the Old Testament days. Clearer somehow.

Satan lives in one of the penthouses on Hypervalue Esplanade, a street name made available for general sponsorship by the city regents, who expected high-end names, the sort of things you get in Formula 1 racing, not detergent companies seeking tax breaks. Mighty Bleach Crescent is the one that forced them to rethink. He invited some rum characters back to his infernal digs, people who want to explore their worst natures. Use your imagination. What sort of party would the Devil throw? Think Marquis de Sade invites the cast of *The Texas Chain Saw Massacre* round for vol-au-vents.

This is a city without its own music, its own style. When you think that three hundred thousand people live here you'd have expected it to carve out more of a niche. But it's no Manchester and it doesn't have a locus such as the

Hacienda which gave birth to the Happy Mondays and unhappier bands too, such as Joy Division, whose lead singer, Ian Curtis was unable to carry the burden of life round the next bend. Liverpool – the Fab Four. Steel Pulse and UB40 giving a reggae beat to Birmingham. Portishead and Tricky make Bristol a mecca for mixers and DJs. But Cardiff, well. The Sound of Silence. That's its theme tune.

There was a time when the huge pubs down the docks such as the Big Windsor hosted nightly R & B, but it was music from somewhere else, played by guys from round the corner. The drummer might live in the flat upstairs and sometimes had barely woken up from a post-beer sleep when he stumbled down to his kit. So, there was no real scene as such. And the Welsh bands who have done well originated in Bethesda or somewhere. Certainly not the city.

In the Bay, in Richard Rogers' glass home for the National Assembly, a conservatory for the people, they're in the middle of a session to decide whether or not to embrace Marina as the official faith of the new nation. It is now seven years since her discovery, and there have been two civil wars because of her and all manner of upsets, but even allowing for those she has still proved to be a mainly benign presence in the world. And the other faiths have made their accommodations. The Hindus know they can have a million more opportunities to improve matters as they are reincarnated over and over again. The Buddhists are in retreat, pardon the pun.

Now that it's had its formal independence there are those seeking to underline the difference between Wales and its imperious neighbour, England. There they can keep that tired Anglicanism, and its High Church antics. Here, in a country which went from being one of the most religious on earth to the most secular in three generations, there's a spiritual vacuum to match an imploded dark star. So Marina has a role to play.

The Presiding Officer gets to his feet and tries to silence the uproarious politicians. He explains that everyone will get a timed ten minutes to make his or her case. This, in itself, sets off eruptions of anger, as representatives of other faiths jostle for attention. They are feeling desperately sidelined by the new cult, with many refusing to call it a religion, even though it now seems to have all the necessary appurtenances – rituals, adherents, a fat bank balance, rapidly acquired arts treasures.

The Islamists make their case quietly, studiously even, making absolutely sure they do not invoke any of the images of burning cars and bombed marketplaces that accompany the notion of their faith in people's minds. In fact the Christians are the most militant and the most threatening. The Bishop of St Davids, dressed in military fatigues and a studded dog collar, has to be physically evicted from the debating chamber by the guards. As he's taken down the front steps they can hear him screaming for justice. The Sikhs argue elegantly but don't have the numbers. The Quakers read out a statement which is beautiful, serene even, and is offered by way of guidance in troubled times. Some New Age druids turn up with their faces dyed cobalt blue with woad, and no one laughs because these are not laughing times. But then the country's

167

representative of the Marinas, a former Queen's Counsel who has debating skills just this side of miraculous, gets to his feet to state quite baldly that there are a million people who espouse the faith in Wales. And there are more joining all the time. Currently there are so many that the Marinas are failing to accommodate the new converts beating a path to their door. He makes a veiled comparison with Scientology, if only to make the point that this is no Johnnie-come-lately faith. It is the same one, he argues, as that which made prehistoric man reach for the stars, or the same need for belief in something which gave Christianity its revival, which raced like gorsefire over the land. Just as the chapels nourished the soul, so too does the new faith. It is shored up by moral precepts. It, too, has a super-natural heart, the attraction of the unexplainable.

And then he reaches for his prop. He brandishes the *Book of Marine Faith*, the fastest selling book in the history of the world, printed by the publishers of *People* magazine in a specially built printing press in Las Vegas, with others to follow in Warsaw and Manila, in which city the architects for the printing press project received an envelope each containing a human ear by way of warning. It might be wise not to build it. Not if you like your ears attached to the head.

As the representative warmed to his theme, the lawyers of the assembly and the civil servants scribbled furiously. This was their world turned upside down. They understood secular matters: they were determined by such forces as fiscal greed and lust for power. But this – this was not in their manuals.

168

The man in front of them, the dazzling lawyer, summoned up all his reserves of oratorical power. He commended the book in front of him as a summation of answers to people's vexations, a compendium of tales and anecdotes wearing the livery of fable and religious utterance, admitting that it was a grand synthesis. It says more about the believers than ever it does about her, but that's not the point. There's something about her that ignites a need to believe, and the first thing anyone has to believe in is her. He believes. In fact he can't begin to understand anyone who doesn't. He draws breath, theatrically:

'In the beginning She was with us, from the opening seconds of the Universe when time's great clock started to mark down, and She will be with us for the last beat, the exploding moment when it all ends not with a whimper, but with the settling of the Great Grey Dust which will envelop all still breathing, settling on our houses and insinuating itself through cracks and under doors. Its drift will be unstoppable, and we shall lie down on the floors with our towels over our mouths and await the end with all dignity, knowing that She is our boon companion, nay She is more than that – she is our perpetual companion, and what lies the other side of time, the other side of our mortal endeavour, is rich because of her, and bearable also.

'There will come that day when breath will be impossible in the dust, but after our extinction, after all memory of our art and science, all our vulgar works, have been entirely expunged, no signs of love, no evidence of palace or stone hut. When every name is erased from memory there will be one that remains. Marina. Who was here and will be here. And when we have finished journeying She will be ready to embark on her great trip. That we have to believe in.'

There were cries of 'Rubbish' and 'Charlatan' and angry fists were waved in the air. The dissenters were ejected, one by one, even though all the people in the chamber knew this was anti-democratic, but they also knew they had to grasp the nettle.

Undaunted, he carried on, gesturing toward the cardinal points as he showed his audience where to look for hope. And then banging his fist over his heart to show where you could find even more hope.

'But for now our faith will be enough, because she is enough, enough to lighten the dark corners, to put hope in the sick child's heart. Because She is a wish fulfilled, She is whatever we want her to be, as She is beyond the reach of our machines and theorems. We may be her own explanation of why she's here. We'll never know. Shepherdess and servant, anchor and teacher, She is all these and more. An unmoving presence who can move us all.'

He rounds off his speech with a plea that *The Book* be a fundamental part of the school curriculum and that each and every child will be encouraged to learn each and every phrase, and be asked to question each phrase and grow up in the sunlight of its refracted wisdom.

'This is a book worth remembering. It's a book I've already learned by heart.'

He finished speaking when his ten minutes was up,

precisely. He wiped his brow with a pure white handkerchief. He almost took an actor's bow.

The Book of Marine Faith was written over eight days in the Holiday Inn in Albuquerque, New Mexico, by: one Nobel prizewinner; two jobbing poets; one former Catholic priest who had been persecuted for defecting to the mongrel faith and had been formally excommunicated by a specially convened Vatican council; three Senegalese fishermen who left their families and their cabins on the beach to follow Her; as well as a US pilot who was looking for a way to deal with the unspeakable things he had done, such as dropping huge payloads of phosphorus on Okinawa during the Second World War. He had read in *TIME* magazine about the woman who arrived in a paper boat and knew by the end of the first paragraph that She held the answer, so he sold his house on the Bay in Maryland and eBayed all his chattels. Within a couple of days he was a man without possessions and left to be Her servant. Sitting next to him in the ballroom was a woman from Rapid Falls, Michigan who had done the same, without understanding her compulsion, but knowing there was only one way she could act, and only one place she could go. Lit by a candle within.

They assembled the book between them. Truth be told, they all contributed, directly.

Each and every pilgrim stood up in front of the hall and spoke into a microphone, talking about their faith, about the effect She had had on them. Many spoke in tongues and others stammered declarations which were sufficiently

171

honest for them to overcome their fear of speaking in public. They gave utterance in many languages, from Italian to Wolof and while some spoke clearly, others used the codes and secret messages of poem and cabal. One predicted a visit to Easter Island. Another that she would replace all minor religions in ten years.

One old lady, who looked as if she should be lying down in a funeral parlour, so pale and wan was she, surprised all and sundry by dancing wildly, transformed into a weightless sprite as she celebrated the Spirit of the Moment. As they all gave witness one of the Massachusetts Institute of Technology's most distinguished recent graduates recorded their testimonies and processed the spew of words into one enormous, confluent text, translating them instantly into Standard English, Spanish and Mandarin (the battle of the languages hadn't been properly fought as yet). His extraordinarily sophisticated software programme looked for the commonalities in what they said, magnifying the echoes and searching for those things that were truly important to each person (analysing stress patterns in their speech, the emphases, the repetitions). He then set them over a bedrock of prayers from world religions, sacred texts from pretty much every culture with a written language. These, all melded together, became the new text, *The Book of Marine Faith,* a great sprawling synthesis, shot throught with the urgency of direct statement. Once it was 'written' it was published, and a major Hollywood star stepped forward to give it its first reading. Everyone in the room could sense how the new words adumbrated their own, as did the Goddess's voice also, if She had one.

172

'In the beginning She was with us and in us . . .' chanted the star, with his salt-and-pepper hair tied back into a tidy ponytail, and as he said the newly minted words the whole of the twenty-first floor at the Holiday Inn wept with impossible happiness as they realized that all present shared one thing which nothing could take away – a faith deeper than the darkest oceanic trench, a hope fit to banish the armies of the world, and a waterfall of love which could sweep the world along with it in a tsunami celebration of the Sleeping One, the Queen of No-Death, the one who came in a fragile craft to show us the way.

By the time the actor had read out the whole book, day had turned into night and back again many times and still they stayed with him, taking comfort breaks only when they really had to and drinking soup that was brought up in huge tureens from the kitchens. Then, after the final words, the star flashed his twelve-million-dollar smile and closed the book with a triumphant thud. Joe Mecks from MIT was saluted and given a tiny fragment of newspaper that had fallen off the side of her boat because he and his ingenious software had managed to create the sort of words that sounded as if they had been carved into tablets of stone, or been born by generations of holy men handing them along collaterally from one generation to the next. He had woven essentials from the Bible, the Qur'an, the Tibetan Book of the Dead and every conceivable theology and account of divine presence in this world to make a verbal tapestry fit to enshroud a new queen.

Joe and his laptop had generated words that had an antique quality and authority which suggested the text had been penned by a monk in a haircloth shirt riddled with fleas, writing determinedly in a cell carved into a honeycomb of rock, by the light of a single guttering candle. Baroque ideas turned into fantastic curlicues, accounts of tempted saints sugared by tales of their spiritual successes. And there was a monk on Joe's screen, generated within the digits of the programme, a hologram that would grace the newest video game, an alter ego for Joe, who is pretty damn agnostic, but feels he needs to have some insight into things. So his totemic monk was modelled on descriptions found in the sort of writings normally seen in chained libraries and creamy parchments in private collections. He was semi-blind from reading by the light of candles he made himself from pig fat. Joe's manufactured 3-D monk was a determined scholar and spent so much time poring over his manuscripts that one day he got up from his stone desk to find he was a hunchback. A little electronic monk, bent over by learning.

In Albuquerque, in the merest instant of computer time, the monk was given nominal authorship of the sacred texts, at the stroke of a key. The manuscripts were adorned with the sort of androgynous creatures that decorate The Book of Kells and the like. The Monsters in the slogan 'Here be Monsters'. A mermaid with a Gorgon's head, with a shock of seaweed hair and a black mamba scarf. A silver turtle with shovel-like claws which looked as if they could dig through the mantle of the earth. An eagle with three heads which flew on silken wings, its talons dripping streams of blood from the twisted carcass of something caught on a crag. And painted among them, Marina, who radiated light and only belonged here because she was unlike anything else, was beyond the insufficient classifications of man. Maybe in the phylum that includes unicorns. Maybe there.

The world's media never let go of the story: it was seldom off the front page, as rabid speculation took over to make up for the paucity of fact. In the multimedia, internet-connected, global village the story of Marina was ripe for expansion and embellishment. There was a massive surge in the number of competing accounts of her birth and early days, and in the dying days of Facebook her page got more hits than all the other addresses put together, and servers everywhere blew up under the strain, overheating from the pressure of data demand. She entranced Second Lifers: old-school builders of SimCity built huge temples and freeways to reach them.

In media hubs and newsrooms on all continents people beavered away to find new things to say about her. Most of them had never seen her in the flesh, if that's what you called the skin that's freckled like pizza dough made of rye flour and pulled tight over her skeleton. Because journalists hardly ever left their desks, other than to go home at end of play. So they spent their time Googling other people's lies and fabrications about the Woman-Who-Sleeps.

There was a welter of competing dates. She was born in Calcutta – before the name change, in Halifax, Nova Scotia, in Cartagena in 1928, 1914, 1939, 1945, and the facts were as solid as a castle built on Marazion sands. But the stuff still got printed, usually unchecked by anyone with an ability to spell, let alone strong ethics when it came to truth, journalists who would trample over feelings with the callousness of a Buru guard, the one with the splinter of ice in his heart.

The latest news story, spreading like a virus across the face of the globe, had more than an inkling or sprinkling of truth, as a Greenpeace spokesperson had alerted the press to a story about a Leviathan which rose up from unfathomable depths to rescue Marina from some evil whalers from the Japanese fleet. This story in itself was enough to slap in place a complete moratorium on whaling. And it was a story already contained in bastardized form in *The Book of Marine Faith*.

In Wales, every empty chapel had been appropriated by the faith. In cities such as Newport, Wrexham, Swansea and Bangor, even some of the bingo clubs had turned from Mammon to Marina, although, truth be told, there was a financial subtext to this. Managers of places such as Gala Bingo had found out that more people came to a New Prayer Morning than to Full House, and they could make more money on religious room rental than ever they could through conventional gaming. Moneymaker Leisure, which owns the greatest number of bingo clubs in the land, went as far as to change the ambient music, piping in Palestrina and John Tavener. They started to illuminate their premises with candles, then scented candles and eventually they started to make candles as a sideline. They had hourly readings from *The Book of Marine Faith* and sang songs about Marina and her voyages.

They started to decorate the converted chapels, which had serious consequences for marine ecologies. Most congregations plumped for a seashore or oceanic theme, and so great stretches of rocky shore were denuded of seaweed. Every single seashell washed up on beach and bluff was taken to adorn a wall or table in Her Honour. In Gerazim in Treborth they made curtains out of strands of dried kelp. In Pisgah, Five Roads, they placed a disused Avon Inflatable liferaft in the *sedd fawr*, the big chair shaped like a half-moon where the deacons would normally sit. The chapel looked like a quayside: there were buoys and a complicated découpage made of razor clams, lengths of barnacle-incrusted hawser, tea chests brought in by the tide.

When millions of jellyfish were blown in to the coasts around Anglesey and the coast of the north west, the believers started referring to this unexpected bounty as 'manna'. The sight of thousands of people beachcombing the rocky inlets from Aberdaron to Porth Neigwl was astonishing, as there seemed to be someone clambering over every overhang. More than one person was put in mind of the Pied Piper of Hamelin and how he made people follow him unthinkingly.

The bacteria-like hordes of humans gathered the profusion of *aurelia aurita* – so we can be sure exactly which species of jellyfish was being scooped into buckets, IKEA bags, wheelbarrows and bin sacks – and despite the fact that they were perfectly edible, disdained even by gulls and skuas. The believers cooked them defiantly – stewed them in the hope they would eventually soften but instead they became as rubbery as the inside of a golf ball, so they ate them more as acts of penance than celebration. It was soup flavoured with belief and that was sufficient for many of them. Some got stung by the nerve agent in the jelly stings and had to be treated at St Lawrence Hospital, Chepstow, which had to close its doors to new patients on three occasions, such was the demand for its services.

Bu there was violence, too, as marauding bands of Christians, Sikhs, Muslims, Hindus, Mormons and all manner of other discarded faiths took up cudgels, picked off stragglers, made themselves awkward. They couldn't believe that time was up for all of them and this casual interloper with her synthetic credos and betrayal of science could usurp them with such oily ease.

The new faith had echoes of voodoo, or vodun, carrying the old beliefs of the Yoruba from their green homelands in Africa to the hellholes of slave-owning America. And one of the new sacred texts bore a great similarity to one of the African myths, and most probably was one of the stories grafted on to the main stem of story by the whizz-kid from MIT.

Olorun, the chief god – who must be obeyed at pain of your child's death – asked Obatala, one of the lesser gods, to create the earth and all living things, such as the Leviathan and dogfish, the jaguar and the snails, creating landmasses that would split into the continents as we know them now and would continue to move and crumble. The god's hands, working like a potter's, would sculpt high peaks and severe trenches, and the waves of his breath would ruffle the waters of the deepest ocean, giving the benthos one last shake before all became dark and his deep-sunken creatures started to change in a hurry.

Jerry Dammers – a preacher man and former carpet salesman who had seen her at rest and had turned his back on the Axminsters and Wiltons once and for all – told the story in the convention in Albuquerque. He told of extraordinary things . . .

'The great sea was the cauldron where Marina mixed all things and separated all things, gave the lobsters the ability to pace the seabed, granted the seals their ululations and the crab its outsize pincers. In the cold beginning, before the lamp of the sun was lit for the very first time, the myriad sea creatures were able to live in harmony, and the sharks would eat nothing but plankton, the whales survived on a diet of processed salt alone, while the little fish were so happy they went without food altogether, and lived on water, feasting their eyes on the kaleidoscope of colour and constant dance of their bright companions.

'A sister goddess, Tonna, was due to carry on the work of creation but she was a bit lazy and slipshod and so she gave to some new species of shark teeth that were too fragile to chew with, and for that mistake she was banished out of the water and was put to live on an island the size of a pocket handkerchief, where she pondered her fate and built up an incredible head of anger. Spite suppurated in her innards and she invented curses to vex and hex once she was off this accursed isle. Some curses worked, such as one she used on the numerous vegetation-stripping river fish, which accounted for the fact that these piranhas like nothing better nowadays than the taste of meat. She made skuas ravenous, and spread a little poison around among blowfish and rock lobster.'

As Jerry Dammers over-egged his preacher's pudding the congregations bayed with enthusiastic interest, driven wild by the story of Marina's devilish shadow.

Marina, be with us! Marina, guide us through life's storms. Be good to us. Look after us!

At the end of the sermon the drums began beating at the back of the houses of worship, and taped sea sounds washed in from the state-of-the-art speakers, and a hologram of Marina was projected in such a way that she could hover just above eye level. The preacher, in an extremely simple but effective piece of ritual, launched a little paper boat into a white ceramic bowl of water, and for some members of the congregation this was quite unbearable so they swooned or wept.

But the new faith didn't prevent anyone else following their own religious paths and so the muezzin still call the faithful to the mosques of Riverside, Grangetown and Tremorfa, and their amplified voices still carry over Sun and Star Street, and other streets called Eclipse, Planet, Comet and Constellation. They rise over Gold and Silver Street and those heavier names, Lead and Zinc. Over the jewel-studded parts of the city their voices dissipate and loop – Sapphire, Emerald, Ruby, Topaz, Diamond and Pearl. And over more mysterious names. Arthur, Blanche and Bradley. Theodora, Harold, Bertram, Cecil, Helen, Nora. Were they friends of the man who built these streets. Or his children?

There are some tribes who refuse to use names at all, as they're seen as being too dangerous, offering the opportunity for theft or misappropriation. And they can be bad in themselves. Ask anyone called Adolf or Judas.

You couldn't ask Jimmie Thomas anything. His head was down, intent, off to make the biggest deal of his life. It was as dark as the inside of a cow's stomach as he set off for an assignation on the edge of East Moors steelworks, between the gipsy camp and the train yard where the new metal ingots leave on wide bogie trucks. Jimmie's daughter can sing. Everyone says so. Therefore, as a responsible father, he was going to give his own little Dusty Springfield her big break.

He'd been sinking them down the Crown when the chance came up. He'd already been to the New Casablanca, the Red Orchid and the North Star, so his blood was a heady cocktail by the time he reached the Crown, a hostelry so rough that they had to rivet the furniture to the floor to stop it being thrown through the windows. Some of the customers were such diehard boozers that they'd had their toes amputated so they could stand closer to the bar. Jimmie'd downed boilermakers at the Glastonbury, sunk Zombifiers at the Stop Tap, guzzled Freaky Ferrets at the Evil Eye and had a Putdowner in a tall glass, no ice at Mad Kit's. Here he witnessed the weekly dwarf-throwing contest, where the vertically challenged man was only too happy to be hurled across the lounge into waiting arms as long as someone was stacking them up at the bar for him. Everyone insisted on buying him a half, as if that was the best joke ever.

But at the Crown he decided to put down roots for a few hours. Drinking wearied him nowadays. Jimmie looked around at the sad prostitutes, whose deathly sallow skin and apple-rouge cheeks made them look as if they were taking part in a pantomime staged in a cemetery. One of them winked at him and winked again until he realized that she had a nervous tic and he looked away. The bar at the Crown was known as the Shooting Range, as you could have any drink you liked in a shot glass and have a whole pint served that way if you chose. According to some it was a more efficacious a way of getting bladdered. Lining up the shot glasses as if there was no tomorrow.

Jimmie was drinking rum in shot glasses, and conversing in the international language of drunks with a crew of old sailors, including an old whaler from the Cape Verde islands who always astonished Jimmie by still being alive, despite the industrial amounts of alcohol he seemed to sluice away each night. He always had a suitcase of conch shells for sale, as well as contraband tobacco, and could mimic whale songs of all species. There was another man who had worked for many years stoking the engines of ships leaving Aden, shovelling coal in punishing temperatures, so that he would have to eat rock salt in between guzzles of water to replace the salt washed out of his pores. He cited that period of labouring in punishing heat, in a ship already overheated by the sun outside, as the root cause of his permanent thirst. His name was Trublood and he was the first to mention him . . . Kenny.

'Kenny went there, you know. Went to meet the Devil down the steelworks. And he had his dream fulfilled . . .'

'What dream?' asked Jimmie, the words jumbling as they tumbled over his lips due to the severe strength of the widowmakers and the boilermakers. 'Which steelworks? What do you mean, the Devil? Do you mean the actual Devil? Oh shit, you know . . .'

Trublood continued, unflustered and genuinely keen to help. He explained how there was a place you could meet Old Nick himself and the deal was as straightforward as it gets. All you had to do was ask for something and offer something right precious in return.

'And this is the Devil himself? Lucifer, you mean?'

'The genuine article. Beelzebub himself. Call him the Great Satan, what you will. He's the one all right. And all he wants is your soul.'

'All?'

The shadows seemed to lengthen and deepen in the room. The light bulbs flickered momentarily. Jimmie tried to form the question on his lips and did so with an almighty effort . . .

'And where is this place?'

Trublood tore the back off a beer mat and licked the tip of a pencil before making a highly stylized drawing.

'Go here. When the moon is full and when you're happy in your mind that the request you have to make is the right request. He'll know you're coming, don't you worry about it.'

Jimmie, despite the oceanic extent of his inebriation, thought Trublood might be more than a little over-dramatic, or maybe clinically insane, but the way in which the other sailors sagely nodded their heads suggested that the Devil was fact, and you could meet him at the crossroads.

This city was full of drunks and most were beyond saving. But there was one drunk you won't be seeing around any more. He was also the first person to be murdered in Marina's name.

In the coroner's court the first case of the week was being heard, to determine exactly how Marky Divotts, a thirty-one-year-old man from St Mellons, died. He had certainly sustained several blows to the head during his last day on earth. It was the court's job to ascertain which of these was the fateful one. It had been a bacchanal, not that Marky would have recognized it as such as he wasn't literate. The time Marky saved on reading he invested in a whirligig existence of toping and violence, the savage drinking leading to equally savage violence, so that he was always wounded, but, as he liked to point out, never as wounded as the other guy. He had a nasty habit of using broken beer bottles in fights and people were naturally very wary of him, especially as his temper had a very low flashpoint. When he did go off it was a real petrochemical explosion and you half expected Red Adair in an asbestos suit.

For seventeen years Marky had lived in a caravan which had dents in the wall where he had lost his rag and holes in the roof where the rain came in. Some of his friends called him Drip because of his home, but only the really hard ones, who could shrug off attacks with shards of broken glass.

Marky drank in some of the same places Jimmie

frequented, although he was also formally banned from all of them. Only his menacing stare got him served in the majority. He usually drank snakebites – a punishing mix of lager and cider – which gave you headaches that were a cross between the pain of neuralgia and having your skull cleft in half by a two-handled axe. An axe wielded by a Swedish berserker, fresh out of the woods, mad with loneliness.

On his last day on earth he'd been standing at the bar with one of Bacchus's most faithful acolytes, the city's last sea captain, now doomed to ferrying cargoes of concentrated orange juice from South America to Cardiff's last working dock. The city had severed itself from the sea by building a barrage to corral the waters of the Taff and Ely rivers. This stupid act had pretty much finished a long history of seafaring. And Captain Evans was the last of the sea captains. But that wasn't his main claim to fame.

Evans was the man who had spotted the Woman-Who-Sleeps in the seas off California. As such he was not only a local but a global celebrity, meaning he was always guaranteed a free drink, so people like Marky stuck to him like a leech when they could.

They were at the Avondale, a salty dive. Evans was regaling all and sundry with the story of how he'd rescued the most famous woman of our times. Every so often he interrupted the telling of the tale so they could watch some poor fucker follow the barman's advice and feed some chicken-flavoured crisps to the fish. The piranhas would try to take his hand off at the wrist and everyone in the pub would fall about laughing, as they always did when an unwitting tourist fell for the prank. Once, a Canadian lost a finger doing it and they'd all had a whip-round and sent him card in the hospital. Another time a woman from the Salvation Army was the innocent dupe, but turned out to be haemophiliac. The water in the tank turned scarlet. There was blood all over the floor and she had fainted clean away by the time the ambulance arrived. When they had a whip-round for her they sent extravagant flowers along with fifty quid for the local Sally Army. But the piranhas loved that moment: it reminded them of a time back in the Amazon when an anaconda had accidentally dropped into a stream. They liked nothing better than a serpent supper. Bonanza!

'Back in the old days,' said the Captain, drawing heavily on his Capstan Full Strength and blowing out the smoke in complete contravention of the smoking ban in public places, 'this place would have been full of seafarers. No one, and I mean no one, had to go without heat as coal was the thing we exported, so coal was the stuff that dockers nicked. They used to be able to steal it and weigh it at the same time so people could put in an exact order, so and so many hundredweights. But now I'm the last one. Soon they'll be bringing people to see me, like dolphins, before I become extinct.'

The old sea captain was reduced to bringing in orange juice from North Brazil with a crew from the Philippines who didn't have a word of English, not even 'Captain'. Together they ploughed through the tempestuous seas of the south Atlantic with the albatrosses in their wake so that orange concentrate could be delivered. A precious cargo?

186

Supermarket juice. How demeaning for a hero. There are those in the pub who remember when Evans ran guns to Bilbao. Not to mention his extraordinary discovery.

In the time it took the Captain to offer this reminiscence Marky had downed four lagers and munched his way through four freebie packs of pork scratchings. He asked for lime cordial in his lager as he kidded himself it was one of his five a day portions of fruit. He had only had a full breakfast for breakfast and he had had to walk across the road to catch the bus into town so he needed to keep up the calories.

Captain Evans was happy to chat about things other than his magical find in the sea. He was sometimes hunted down by some real nutters who were obviously haunted by that story. Despite the fact that all this had happened years previously she still appeared in new tattoos, bits of graffiti, Marina church openings and she was still easy fodder for the online newspapers. At one stage Evans was himself dogged by paparazzi, as if there was something special about him beyond being the chance discoverer of a woman in a boat.

'Woooooyewlikeanother?' slurred Marky through a gob full of greasy pig dermis.

The Captain said he'd adore another whisky and hinted it didn't have to be a small one. He took off his captain's hat to scratch his head. A group of local detectives came in for a couple of quiet tranquillisers and to process the latest crime to pass over their desks. The Captain nodded at them as they turned into a huddle to talk about terrible murders and blunt weapons.

'We are here,' said the coroner clearing his throat, 'to decide how the late Mark Lancelot Divotts died. I'd like to start by inviting the pathologist to report.'

The pathologist had an unfortunate surname, Dr Weevil, and he started by listing a few basic statistics. Heart, three hundred grammes. Liver condition, sclerotic. Genitalia normal.

'I could have told him that,' came a stage whisper from the centre of the court. It was Marky's common-law wife, Poppaline, with the emphasis on common. There were titters of embarrassed laughter. Marky's wife had used so much spray on her hair that she looked like something out of a B-movie, a real fright. The Gorgon of Llandeilo. Looked like she'd used superglue to perm her hair. A whole tub of it, applied with a stick.

She'd dressed her sexy best, though, with her limitless skills for luring a man put to best use. After all, Marky used to pay the bills, and with him gone she'd need a sugar daddy. Sizing up the various men in court she dismissed the coroner as being too old and obviously faithful with it. She never could explain her gift but within seconds of meeting a man she could tell whether or not he would betray his wife.

The court usher had a permanent leer on his face, although his body odour was in its way triumphant, an overpowering musk that made you want to retch. Still, he probably drew a regular salary and that was worth the occasional hurl and, besides, you can grow accustomed to pretty much anything, given time. She winked at him and he winked back after making damned sure there wasn't anyone else watching.

The pathologist was tidying up loose ends, stating categorically that Mr Divotts had died because of a blow to the skull, which had occasioned a haemorrhage.

The coroner thanked Dr Weevil who sat down to listen to the rest of the session. He didn't do this as a rule, but he was intrigued by the deceased's wife, who had the sort of in-your-face attitude that got him going. He found her raunchy beyond.

'It is likely that the late Mr Divotts fell or was knocked on the head on several occasions during an extended drinking session. His blood alcohol content was extraordinarily high, and he might well not have reacted to some of these blows in the same way a sober man would, staggering on, no doubt. In fact I should record that I have not encountered such levels of alcohol in forty years, and the pathologist, as you heard, was likewise surprised.'

Pretty much everything in the city was recycled nowadays, what with the globe-saving attitude of the local council, which had a zealot's energy when it came to avoiding landfill and aiming for zero waste, like New Zealand. There were also the patrolling hordes of freelance waste collectors who could rescue pretty much any broken object and give it new life. Strimmer was one such operator and he specialized in rescuing video games, computers, mobile phones, that sort of thing, which had been discarded in leafy suburbs such as Rhiwbina and Lisvane, and then making them work again. It was like those Indian cities you read about in the Sundays, where nothing is discarded and everything is a source of work. Phones were the most desirable objects, and Strimmer just had to clean them up before selling them on. With phones he knew how to hook up with someone else's account for a week at a time, so he could offer as many free minutes as ASDA.

Strimmer used to work as a gardener, but he finds rooting through skips just as satisfying in its own way. Some skips he has to fight over, but he's handy with his fists just as he is with his hands when they're unclenched. If there is a fallow period when the city's skips are empty, he steals. If he loses his nerve stealing he turns to the homeless charities, who'll usually sub him a few bob, put a roof over his head. He hates hand-outs though, and things have to come to a pretty pass for him to drink so much free soup. He is naturally a worker not a shirker and so he'll work if he can.

Things had been going his way these past few months. He woke up in a lime-green world, as he was renting a bedsit painted in garish colours, so that he sometimes felt as if he was trapped in someone else's hallucination. Before breakfast, which didn't feel like breaking a fast, seeing as he had a couple of death kebabs at two in the morning when he was coming back from a round of skips, he watched some home-made porn: he'd dubbed the audio from a couple of Welsh-language cooking programmes on to a sequence of graphic images of intercourse edited together by a jilted former lover of Strimmer's ex-girlfriend, and featuring the girlfriend in various contortionist poses. The images were both explicit and wounding, if a little

190

stimulating, truth be told. He made sure to send her a copy, along with all of her friends and a lucky bag for her boss in the bank. The chef's words seemed hysterical in the new context, especially when he started to extol the virtues of keeping the chicken head to boil down to make stock. It was just Strimmer's mind of course, down at sewer level. But as he pondered the kitchen vocabulary in this context a thought came to him. A eureka moment!

An hour later he was down the Army Surplus Emporium buying fishing gear, lengths of netting, sacks, ropes and bags of tent pegs, as if he was going to pitch camp for himself and a hundred mates, as well as purchasing assorted bags of seed and a full set of camouflage fatigues, complete with stormcoat and overtrousers. He looked as if he could pass for shadows in the Burmese jungle.

The next morning he wasted no time, getting up before the larks and the refuse men. He drove down to Brannigans bakery where he gave his friend Jock ten quid to let him into the back yard. He set up the traps as deftly and effortlessly as if he'd been doing this all his life. Squirrels and pigeons came to the back of the bakery in their hordes to pick over spilled grain and discarded pastry mix. When the delivery lorries backed out there'd often be a considerable spillage just of crumbs which had been shaken loose as the trays were loaded. Strimmer felt certain his simple traps would work and that soon his sacks would be full to the brim. It took just an hour and half for him to catch a dozen collared doves and two squirrels that became frantic in the nets. He dispatched them all with a solid six-inch bludgeon, stoving in their skulls with ease and unexpected skill.

He was finished before the night shift left and even managed to pluck the birds and skin the squirrels, so that when he went over to see his friend Cenith he was ready to open for business. Cenith was going to rent him the burger van, had even thrown in a couple of huge plastic bags full of baps to get him going. He'd also knocked up a basic marinade using several herbs and lemon juice; it sloshed around in Tupperware containers.

The menu said guinea fowl kebabs but the doves from the bakery made excellent substitutes. As he'd caught a few starlings and a couple of thrushes he decided to offer quail and partridge as well. He was so confident that he had the right sort of merchandise he dispensed with taking ketchup with him on his first outing, to a football game in a very minor league, where there were only fourteen spectators but he sold thirty-one baps. Do the math. A roaring trade.

A gibbous moon, pregnant with creamy light, was suspended over the skyline. Jimmie walked his long shadow toward the docks, his haversack filled with beer flagons, his stomach filled to the pit with worry. He came from a very religious family – his grandmother not only believed that her Saviour lived but that he lived in Adamsdown. But Jimmie didn't believe in God, so found it strange that he should believe he was on his way for an assignation with the Devil. The moon bothered him. Did the Devil come out on moonless nights?

He walked purposefully past lines and lines of coal

trucks, the wheel rims lit in bright outline. Ten minutes to go and his heart was racing along like a disco anthem. A bottle of beer, downed in one, helped calm him a fraction. His teeth, the back molars, hurt where he'd used them to take the top off the bottle. It was a useful distraction. When he could see the crossroads in the distance, luminescent as if spotlit, he opened another beer, but this time used a rock to knock off the metal top. He also emptied his bladder, though his hands were shaking as if he had palsy. Then he moved into the shadows to observe. Nothing happened.

Each stride had taken it out of him, as if this were physical exertion. At the appointed place he debated with himself whether or not he should call out. There was no protocol for this. His heartbeat thumped like a primitive drum and he was afraid that it was audible for miles around. Shadows moved like snakes as willow branches moved in front of the arc lights of the railway sidings, while ribbony shadows fled away from the moon in the opposite direction. Jimmie looked all around him, his mouth dry now and his skin clammy with fear. He looked at his watch, the numerals lighting up a ghastly glow. Then a man appeared, or at least the shape of a man, but this one had a horrible hiss in lieu of a voice. It had a dampness to it, like methane. And Jimmie would later relate how he could smell a hint of sulphur. Maybe he used brimstone aftershave.

'Jimmie, Jimmie, Jimmie,' said the marsh-gas voice. It was as if he were savouring the name and playing with its owner at one and the same time. The smell of his breath intensified and wrapped around the heavy stockman's coat the man was wearing like a heavy feather boa, the sort of thing that's made out of whole ostrich.

Jimmie was dumbstruck. This was an apparition. He sought in vain for a face, something to latch on to. But there was just darkness and vacancy and these were more terrifying, like peering into a bottomless abyss. Jimmie'd seen a lot of images of the Devil but this one didn't square with any of them: no cloven hooves, no red tail, no horns, no triangular beard, no trident, no goat fur, and he couldn't even be sure of the sulphur smell, which he could probably put down to imagination. Yet he knew with all his heart that this was the Devil.

The wind had stilled and the willow branches frozen into place. Clouds had devoured the moon. A chill settled in Jimmie's bones as he began to make out the Devil's words, spoken in a voice that had all the reassurance of a child-murderer reading out the school register. Jimmie's drum kept time with them.

'What do you want Jimmie? Tell me what you really want, Jimmie.'

The sing-song was monstrously unsettling but at least Jimmie had an answer ready.

'I have a daughter and I want her to use her voice. She has a great voice, the voice of an angel.'

'Don't be coming round here with talk of angels, Jimmie. You should know better. They're a plague, they are.'

'I want her to sing so well that all the world will hear her,' Jimmie persevered. 'Her voice is pure velvet and it's like no other.'

'Said with a father's galling affection, Jimmie. And why should I grant you this favour. What's in it for the dark side?

'I, I, I . . .'

'Don't stammer, Jimmie. It's a sign of weakness, or at the very least indecision. Let me make it simple for you. All you have to do is cut your name in my little black book and then it's a deal struck as if we'd done so in blood. Not that I have any blood in my veins and no veins to speak of, although I do have plenty of blood on my hands. Think Congo, man, or Iran-Iraq. Such plentiful bloodlettings.'

'And she will entrance audiences the whole world over? You can guarantee this?'

'She surely will. Sure as eggs is eggs. Here take this, put your signature anywhere you like. I'm sure there's a clean page in there somewhere.'

'And will this happen in my lifetime, I mean will I be able to go and hear her sing in a concert somewhere?'

'I don't see why not. After all, you are giving me your eternal soul.'

Put that way the deal seemed to Jimmie a little lopsided. 'Eternal' was troubling in this context. He took the book and signed on a page that featured just a few other names. Quite a few Evanses due to its being such a popular surname. And the fact that it was a family given to thievery.

'She's going to bewitch them, believe you me,' said the Devil with extra hiss. 'She'll have recording contracts – probably with Sony – limousines, perfectly chilled champagne for breakfast and fans that will swoon at the very mention of her name. There'll be awards, plaudits, her name on the front pages and eligible men beating a path to her door.'

Then the Devil disappeared and the breeze soughed in again and the clouds were banished, as if a freeze frame had thawed. There was the fat moon and there was Jimmie, sitting on the floor, winded by the experience. His body seemed out of control, paroxysm following paroxysm of pain and relief and the drum inside his ribcage feeling as if it was breaking free.

In their spanking new offices and studios overlooking the Norwegian Church in Cardiff Bay the *Byd ar Bedwar* team was preparing its latest Welsh language current affairs programme. They were all relieved after the special about the effect of Marina on the Assembly had been so well received, even by the heads of other faiths. Some of the journalists were tired of doing stories about her, but luckily the audience's appetite seemed finally to be sated. The rate of conversion to the new faith had also stabilised as if the optimum had been reached. The senior hacks were hacked off because the programme no longer came under current affairs but was now classified as light entertainment, so audience numbers counted for far more than journalistic probity or the thoroughness of the investigation.

Take a look at the set for the show to see how that works – it was all jazzy light sequences and musical items to leaven the serious stuff. And the key word was *confrontation*, and if that could be live confrontation all the better, so the show had descended to depths even the late Jerry Springer would not and could not condone, or stoop to.

The new producer liked to add a touch of cruelty to the proceedings and it was fitting that her name was Lucrezia, Lucrezia Mantol, who hailed from Millwall's Isle of Dogs. She had been chair of the football supporters there, notorious for their propensity to use hatchets on other fans, and given to violence that was almost abstract in its intensity. Ironically, she owed her spell in prison to another TV programme, *World in Action*, which dogged her every step for months, but without alerting her. Professionals. Managed to film her kicking a supine Darlington player in the head.

While she was in Selly Oak Prison in the West Midlands she shared a cell with a lass called Catrin ap Huwcyn, a member of Cymal 30, a Welsh-language extremist group which believed in using pretty much any tool available to them to stem the flow of incomers into *Y Fro Gymraeg*, those areas of Wales where the language was strongest, but still in a mightily precarious position.

Catrin's own personal modus operandi was kidnapping the pets of influential people and then torturing them in front of a camera before demanding whatever it was that she and the rest of Cymal were demanding at the time. Sometimes it was just an explicit request that the white settlers should remove themselves from a village in *Y Fro* within an allotted time frame. It was curious that holding up a poodle to the flame of a blowtorch seemed to be as efficacious as holding kids to ransom. They'd kidnapped one child whose parents went on holiday despite seeing the ransom request. But the family pet, well . . .

Catrin's comeuppance followed an audacious and

bloodily cruel heist in which Cymal not only snatched a Jack Russell dog from its home but sent a paw to its distressed owners, who had committed the crime of buying up six houses in the village of Abersoch to use as holiday lets, essentially gazumping any local people who wouldn't have had the money to compete against such well-heeled opposition. An eagle-eyed Post Office worker had spotted the blood seeping out of the parcel and they'd tracked its history.

During her eighteen-month stint in the cells, Lucrezia learned Welsh from Catrin while Catrin was taught such skills as how to forge a document, using software available to all who knew where to look. Lucrezia also taught her advanced kung fu and how to make Molotov cocktails like the ones they'd once used to set ten Spurs supporters on fire.

It doesn't take much to get some of the criminals to turn up at the studio for an unmasking. There are those, such as the senior police officers they featured some months back, who are a stupendous combination of preternaturally stupid and preeningly vain. Dumb-ass loan sharks fall for versions of the same scams they themselves perpetrate. Ministers of the cloth fall for smooth-talking researchers, duped into revealing their peccadillos with members of the congregation and speaking pretty much directly into hidden lapel cameras. The studios' lawyers have also found a fabulous loophole in the law which allows the TV confession, even if obtained by subterfuge and deceit, to be admissible as evidence in a court of law. So the audience sits in on the equivalent of a cop-shop interview room and the police could, should they wish, arrest interviewees on set. This helps mitigate the effects of highlighting the misdemeanours of senior police in previous episodes.

The loophole was this. There had to be a complete record of the interview and tapes of the programme were allowable as just that. And the do-badder had to have deep pockets to compete with the deep-pocketed legal fighting fund of the telly people. So they kept on making programmes and the brain-dead box watchers out in TV-land kept on watching. A third of them were Marinas by now.

Lucrezia had pulled together all staff to work on their special programmes. The live audiences were pre-booked, and they'd had to deal with a solid flow of requests to sit in the purple plastic seats. They got the IT folk to work out a new way of garnering an audience vote, on a system which mimicked Imperial Rome, a thumbs down and a thumbs up arrangement, which neatly underlined the gladiatorial nature of it all. They recorded trails which promised viewers 'unequivocal truth and nothing less' and these were due to be aired every twenty minutes or so at peak time on the channel. The chief reporter, Luke Thomas, said he had a candidate in mind for next week's show, a man called Steven Thomas, known familiarly as Strimmer. The other Thomas promised it would be like a devilish version of a cookery show. Some of the company executives who'd sat in on the production meeting smacked their lips in anticipation of the viewing figures. Thomas explained what was in Strimmer's sandwiches and how many vans he had on the road at the moment and how he'd just been given a whopping business development grant, a mighty whack of government money, which made the whole thing a matter of public interest. Lucrezia apportioned their various tasks and they all set to work with alacrity.

In the lime-coloured flat, Strimmer counted the money his vans had taken outside the Bluebirds game against West Bromwich Albion, where he'd been trialling their latest marketing slogans, which were designed to appeal to innate Welshness and a man's love for his mother. *Like mam's home cooking. All Welsh inside.* Even skinhead thugs seemed to respond favourably. They ate enormous amounts of heavily spiced vermin both before and after the game.

Strimmer totted up the actual sales: they had shifted nearly eight hundred feral pigeons which, he reckoned, helped save a heck of a lot of bird shit on the city streets. He'd caught these by applying lime on to the netting designed to keep the birds away from the undersides of railway bridges: he'd paid two skinny whippet lads to scale the brickwork in order to bring down them down, which needed a degree of abject cruelty, as their legs were stuck to the metal. You had to tear them off, leaving two stalk-legs behind. Such easy money! He'd started to buy stale bread from four bakeries, which was more than enough to pull in his prey to the usual traps. He'd stopped renting the vans and was now the proud owner of what was shaping up as a whole goddamn fleet of them.

Strimmer phoned up his best friend, Doug, who was blessed with a cast-iron stomach and had eaten all manner of things on his peregrinations around the world with the army. He had eaten spider monkey brains using small silver spoons in Guatemala. Skinned racoon in the Adirondacks. He'd cooked marmot stew and tasted the sphincter of a bull, served on a toothpick. Strimmer asked Doug if he was game for a visit to the sewers and his mate asked him why exactly? A tentative grin crossed his friend's face.

'To appreciate the extraordinary architecture.'

Strimmer was planning to extend the menu in a particularly unsavoury direction and was out to get rats. He and Doug would get a chance to admire some fine tiling and impressive engineering as they did so.

The *Byd ar Bedwar* journalists listened to the wiretap recordings and knew they needed to get some filmed material and so by the time Strimmer and Doug showed up in the lock-up off Tyndall Street they were waiting in an unmarked van with tinted windows, cameras at the ready. They were so adept at what they did that Strimmer didn't have a clue.

Little did the shoppers on Queen Street and Saint Mary Street know about the underworld beneath their feet. The genius of the Victorian age was expressed in various edifices and built expressions above ground but the ill-smelling catacombs under the main shopping streets and older parts of town were perhaps the finest expressions of a desire to combine functionality with decoration. The same instinct that gave London its St Pancras, the regal chain of South Kensington museums and the Midland Grand Hotel created the cloacal networks which shunted the faeces of thousands of Cardiff denizens down to the

201

sea. Strimmer and Doug wore clothes pegs over their noses as they lifted up a manhole cover to descend into the nether reaches of the system. Strimmer had a map and a bit of recent intelligence about where to go.

As their headlamps scanned around the tunnels they did indeed see some pretty amazing features. In one place the variously coloured brickwork was arranged to look like a dawning sun, and in another a galaxy of stars turned in faded nebulae. There was even a fresco which told the story of Josiah Cardiff, who gave the city its name and was the first multimillionaire in Britain by all accounts. It gave the two men pause.

Josiah Cardiff was born Josiah Bertram Evans, the son of a holy union between a worker in the copperworks and a seamstress, and entered the world in Constellation Street in Splott, or God's Plot, in 1820, exactly a year after the birth of Queen Victoria. In so many ways his life paralleled hers. Not in privilege, perhaps, but certainly he mirrored her vaulting ambition and gift when it came to commanding people to bow to her will. Josiah was a moderately gifted pupil in school, picking up his tables and his reading without any problem, although the stern regime of discipline got his hackles up. He was regularly punished for his rebellious streak and disregard for authority. Even as a youngster he believed people had to earn respect. The headmaster, with those terrible boils on his nose which looked like the bulbs of spring onions, hadn't earned one iota of it. Not a jot. But Josiah's true gifts lay hidden and unbidden during all of his formal schooling, if you can dignify it with such a description. More beating than learning.

He gained an apprenticeship with a ship chandler in Butetown where he enjoyed the parade of colourful old salts who came through the doors, but there was one more colourful than all the rest, namely one Henry Erasmus Cardiff, who designed ships for the Royal Navy. The story was famous by now about his coming into the store and noticing the young lad designing a system for moving goods around. Preserved meats, bottles of grog and heavy clothing zinged along a network of overhead wires courtesy of an ingenious system of pulleys and tripswitches which he'd made himself from odds and ends. It was ingenious beyond, but Henry particularly appreciated the extra details, such as the little brass tags the boy had made which carried the prices of each of the items. This did away with the need for ledgers, and indeed for some of the imperious-minded clerks who filled so many desks at other similar companies. Josiah had evident gifts, that was for certain.

Henry offered him an apprenticeship that very afternoon. He accompanied the lad to see his father as he finished his shift at the copperworks. The old, tired man was staggered to see Josiah step out of a grand coach as if he always travelled in such style. He was a perceptive old man. A wave of dismantling sadness passed through him as he realized that the boy would soon be leaving them. Within minutes he was being made a cash offer for his son's services, amid discussion of the various advantages that would come in the wake of all this. Henry was a polished performer, used to bringing people round to his way of thinking. But Josiah's dad was a pragmatist: he had the pragmatism of a poor man who has beaten the system and made his own way in the world. He knew what was best for his son and just checked with him that he was ready for this change in his life, then gave his unequivocal blessing.

As the three concluded their business they watched whole families turning up with the contents of their nightpots. They were paid for their urine, which was used in the coppermaking process, and so it was worth them having a pot to piss in. Urine was more valuable than water. The two men shook hands, and Henry ushered his new apprentice back into the carriage, which left with a great clatter of horses' hooves. The iron on stone echoed like buckshot.

'Would you like to be an architect?' asked Henry as they headed for his house. 'And an engineer?'

The boy assented with a nod, even though he didn't have the foggiest what an architect was.

They had arranged to pick up his things that very evening and took a trunk with them. This proved entirely unnecessary as the boy's chattels in life were few in number and could have fitted into Dick Whittington's handkerchief. It was agreed that the parents could visit him whenever they wished and that Josiah would go home on alternate Sundays, although that arrangement would soon break down as the lad took to his new life and started to negotiate the silvery paths of his privileged education. Besides, the working class didn't cross social boundaries very easily: the parents were most unlikely to drop round for a cuppa. A cup of tea served in exquisite porcelain, handed to them without a tremor by the gloved hand of a consummate butler. That wouldn't be happening in a hurry.

Josiah took to his new life with zeal. He saw the servants as friends and was forgiven by Henry for not placing sufficient distance between himself and them: they liked him for his openness and regard for their health and well-being. They liked their old master as well, for he was courteous to a fault and looked after his staff, even when they were ill or incapacitated.

As for Josiah's education, Henry decided to take care of that himself, with the help of an array of tutors, so that they could go at his protégé's pace, which was a fair lick indeed. A Hungarian mathematics tutor managed to teach him theorems and equations that Oxford graduates would have found baffling, despite having an accent that was well-nigh impenetrable to the ears of the young lad. By the time he was sixteen Josiah was able to turn out detailed architectural drawings and had studied the work of some of the world's finest engineers. He had an eye for detail and an aptitude for practical solutions. Some of the tutors used words such as 'flair' and 'panache' to describe the young student. Indeed there was something dashing, but not slapdash, about his exercises. He was forever designing boats, launching an endless fleet of ideas.

The day came when Josiah not only designed his first seagoing craft but saw it built of wood and metal, thereby setting the foundations of a mighty naval force that would commandeer the world's oceans, enabling Britain to keep its iron grip on the farthest reaches of the world. And in Josiah's case the word 'iron' adumbrated his incredible future as he was to design the mighty *Dreadnought*, the first warship to be made entirely of iron, which helped allow a small set of islands to police all seven seas. 'Rule Britannia, Britannia Rule The Waves'. Curiously, this candidate for an alternative national anthem was penned by Thomas Arne with Josiah in mind. Arne was an old college chum of Cardiff's. The lad liked hearing the poem set to various tunes, finding it rousing in most versions. Josiah was magnetized by the heroic in life.

A few weeks before the launch of the *Deadnought* in Greenwich Mr Cardiff summoned his protégé to the drawing room. There was an unusual seriousness to his guardian's demeanour. At first Josiah thought he must have done something wrong, something to upset him.

'You have been like a son to me these past years,' said the old man, leaning forward in his leather chair. 'I cannot tell you how satisfied I am with your progress: you have a future ahead of you that I can only begin to imagine. You are already a proven scholar and your gift for design is unparalleled. Respect and admiration are yours, and there are those who already mention you as the most learned man in the land despite the fact that you are only twenty-one. Your first visit to a Cambridge college was to lecture there: now fancy that! I haven't asked anything of you in all the time you've been under my care, but I've reviewed your stipend each year so that we're both clear about the nature of our relationship. Now, I have something to ask of you. Two things, in fact.

'As you know I had a wife who died years before her time. She died minutes after the birth of a son who was strangled in the womb. The years that followed were years of darkness and abject misery: there were times I wanted to walk out into the tides, let me confess. But hard work was my salvation and I gave myself over to it entirely. I still visit their graves but increasingly I do so out of a sense of duty not of regret. The biting pains that tore at my insides have diminished over time and will I'm sure one day disappear completely. I can now think of them with fondness, and the ache of absence is something which is almost, well, comforting. Then you came along and have taken a central place in the expedition that is life. Now I find that my purpose is to look after you and nothing else. To that end I want to ensure you're well provided for when I have passed on and should like to formally take you on as my ward. I wish to talk to your parents about these matters but first I need your blessing. Will you accept me as your guardian?'

'Yes, of course, father. It has been an honour to study under you, to see the world at your side. I have learned so much and want to learn so much more.'

'But there is one more thing. I want you to take my name. I want you to be Josiah Bertram Cardiff. It's not ownership, just simple, unadulterated pride. How does that sound – Josiah Cardiff?'

'It sounds like the name I've always carried. It would be a matter of impossible pride to carry your name. And I'm sure my parents will agree. Their pride shines like a star.'

The lad touched his forelock in salute.

'There'll be no need for any of that anymore. We shall be equals. Righty-ho. I'm going to pen a letter to your parents right this minute and arrange to see them post-haste. I'd like to get this sorted before the launch if I can.'

The ship's launch was a pageant of colour and a display of extraordinary military might, with enough artillery to destroy the Isle of Wight. Brass bands lined the dockside and stands had been erected for all the dignitaries. Josiah held his breath as she slid down the rollers, floating on the water like a great grey goose. His calculations had been correct, after all!

Mr Cardiff and Josiah's mam and dad shook hands, the three of them beaming mightily with pleasure. The *Dreadnought* was a towering achievement, quite literally. *The Times* would describe Josiah as a wunderkind, suggesting he was the new Isambard Kingdom Brunel. The papers piled on the superlatives and this in an age of superlatives.

Two years later Josiah Cardiff designed a warship twice as big as the *Dreadnought*. Twice the size and yet twice as fast. The Navy volunteered to call it the HMS *Cardiff*.

Josiah went on to design a railway that crossed Scotland, and he created the first ever workable submarine, not to mention pioneering experiments with materials that would later be recognized as the beginning of the manufacture of plastics. In the city of his birth he was celebrated for creating the gargantuan warship, and after his death it was exhibited in the Royal Dock, where for years it was the most dominant shape on the skyline. That was until a world war increased demand for scrap metal and she was sent for smelting. A guilty city pondered how it might continue to honour its most famous son and struck upon a wizard idea. They decided to name the city after him. So he would live on in memory as long as the city stood. Jamestown. Washington. Cardiff. All these places named after men. There are those named after women, too. Athens, Charlotteville and, of course, a plenitude of Victorias. Not to mention Alice Springs.

Strimmer and Doug stared at much of this legend depicted in brick hieroglyphs in front of them – a ship being launched, a submarine, a train among pines – stories told in silence under the city streets. They moved on, setting traps filled with fresh cow liver along the walkways which connected the main tunnels. They only had to wait for twenty minutes before a wild gnashing of teeth and unearthly, bitter squealing told them they had caught their first rats who were busy murdering each other in the confines of the traps.

The clothes pegs on the men's noses were proving powerless against the mightiness of the stench. The sight of the throng of rodents driven wild by the smell of wet meat, not to mention the plashing spectacle of them ploughing through water speckled with little pellets of faeces took their minds off the cloying smell, if only momentarily. The two sewer-hunters found themselves in a frenzy of blood as they took out struggling rats, blessing the heavy falconer's gloves they were wearing. The best way of killing them was simply to bash the back of their heads against the brickwork. They filled three sacks in less than an hour, taking the bodies back up through the manhole, thence back to the lock-up to be skinned and cleaned.

Strimmer had a blemmer of a recipe lined up for them. It had been given to him by no less a figure than the First Minister himself, who said that nothing could rival properly prepared *cuy*, or guinea pig.

Strimmer had found a recipe in a library book called *Hot Food From the Andes*. It seemed easy to follow. In the photograph he couldn't see what the difference would be between a rat and a guinea pig. Not covered in sauce, anyway. Fresh rat, sourced locally!

Cuy bought in a local market will usually be already skinned, but they are easy to prepare yourself. You start by washing the cuy *in hot water, then pull out the innards and wash the body thoroughly using salted water. You can then hang it to drain and dry. As cuy is a small animal you will need at least one per person unless you intend to cut the meat finely. Usually it is necessary to split the body down the middle and then cook it whole, keeping the head on, although some people don't like to see the little teeth smiling at them on the plate (though most Peruvians treat the head as a delicacy in its own right).*

You will need . . .

3 or 4 cuys (fat ones, if possible: ask your merchant to reserve some)

50 grammes of roast wheatgerm, or india corn

2 kilos of potatoes, parboiled and then cut into chunks (reserve cooking water)

8 garlic cloves (or to taste, some people crave five times that much garlic!)
6 fresh peppers, red or yellow, cut into strips, de-seeded
Half a cup of oil
Half a cup of water
Salt, pepper and cumin

Rub the cuy *with a mixture of salt, pepper and cumin and then roast it (you can also cook it over a barbecue). Both techniques take less time than you think and you don't want the meat to be dry. Ten minutes in the oven or five over open coals.*

Prepare the sauce by combining the oil, peppers, garlic, india corn and water from the potato pan. Cook for four or five minutes until the peppers have softened nicely. Place the meat in a pan and cover with sauce. Serve with the potatoes on the side.

Decorate with green leaves, coriander, basil, whatever is to hand.

Strimmer followed the recipe to the letter, other than substituting rats for the *cuys* and cutting down on the oil and peppers. And having to decapitate the animals. Their teeth would make them easily recognisable otherwise.

The next round of traps, nicely fortified and rendered attractive to *rattus norvegicus* by leftovers from Chunky E. Chicken and the Tastealot café in Canton was a roaring success. Strimmer was able to freeze enough for every rugby international fixture in the coming season. He took sackloads back to the unit on the industrial estate where he had just started to prepare a new line in oven-ready food served in foil containers. The new curries could conceal a host of mischiefs. He had started to think of dogs, and wondered where he could get a supply. Cats, now, he was sure he could arrange those himself. Now that he had the trapping skills of a contemporary Daniel Boone, his company, Tasty Bargain, could go far. Plus he had the government money, which they'd bent over backwards to give him. Couldn't speed up the payments process enough. He already had two new trucks on order, which he'd paid for out of the proceeds of a new contract to supply old people's homes in Carmarthenshire. He hoped they liked grey squirrel bolognese. Heavy on the onions.

Pride fills a father like a balloon, so that he almost levitates over the audience in front of him. Jimmie was watching his little girl onstage. She was singing like a skylark, the helium notes soaring, cut free from gravity. The judges seemed to be relishing her performance. She had exemplary stage presence and a sassy self-confidence. She was clearly her own woman which made her stand out from the other contestants, who slavishly imitated people in the Top Twenty.

The setting was St David's Hall and these were the Wales and West of England heats of *Mad with Talent*. Whoever won tonight went through to the final at the London Palladium plus they get the chance to win a million pounds and embark on a world tour which takes in Carnegie Hall, the Sydney Opera House and a whole host of other prestigious venues. Doreen looked to be well up on points when she entered the final ballad round. Eleven points in the lead, and the only real contender a young kid with a voice that seemed strained to the outer limits by the songs he's chosen.

Jimmie almost swooned when he saw his baby doll in her new outfit, which she'd selected that very morning in a dress shop with royal connections. Doreen was a vision in aubergine, and her hair swished like the woman in the Timotei shampoo commercial.

For the next song her enunciation was perfect, her composure absolute, her stage presence magnified as if she was older than her years. She could also sustain a note like a diva, even though she had never had a breathing lesson in her life. Her final note sounded as if it might last into the middle of November.

One morning, Doreen had woken up with a miraculous voice and an ability to use it. It had a slightly exotic quality, sounding as if it had travelled far to reach her, like a swallow that's worked hard, battled headwinds to make landfall. By that afternoon she was listening to her voice filling spaces in a way its wan, effete predecessor could never hope to do. She could control the melody with surety, and add emotional inflection fit to break your heart.

The judges gushed their praise. They were beaming like idiots, entranced by one of the best performances they'd ever witnessed.

'Let me make it absolutely clear. You *are* the next big thing. That was entirely delightful. You made the song your own. Your owned the audience. The most wonderful thing we've had on the series. Ever.'

'Darling, that voice is worth more than a million

213

pounds. It's worth all the gold in the world. What am I saying? It *is* solid gold.'

'Brilliant. Dazzling. Ella. Aretha. Dusty. All rolled into one. You'll go as far as you want to go.'

Bouquets of flowers rained down on the stage. The little girl cried. Her father thought all the blood vessels in his body were going to explode.

And of course, three weeks later, in front of a global TV audience of over forty million she sang her way to glory, with a version of 'Say a Little Prayer' which she commandeered and steered to a new place altogether. It was, in its way, audacious. Covering an Aretha song. But then to refashion it as if it was newly minted! People wept in the studio. Families shuddered with emotion at home. Doreen dismantled them. She bloody pulverized them with the power and nakedness of her voice.

There had been a good few hopefuls who had beaten a path to meet the Devil to ask for similar favours, all willing to pay the extraordinary asking price. Uncles had stood there, vain aunts, desperate mothers, so many in fact that Old Nick was thinking of opening up an infinite number of concert halls in hell so that there could be endless awful music. He'd have to place an order for bigger ledgers. A2, maybe.

He remembered one hopelessly optimistic fucker who wanted a two-for-one deal for his twins, not realizing that with only one soul to trade nothing whatsoever was possible.

Another man made a far more modest proposal concerning his dying son, asking that he be allowed to play with Bob Dylan's house band. The Devil thought it was an excellent trade-off as he only had to wait for a fortnight before the tumour accelerated to the pancreas and he could put a thick black tick next to another name. He reminded himself to get someone to steal another box of pencils. BB, he liked a soft graphite tip. Maybe a gross of them, as things were getting busy. He was killing time before the Woman-Who-Sleeps arrived, amassing quite a tally.

The court heard about one blow after another. They seemed to rain down on Marky's bonce.

In Dempsey's he'd brought it on his own head, and it hurt. He'd told the barman that he was such an appalling runt because he, Marky, was his actual father and had sired him in an alleyway in Llangennech with his mother, who really wasn't choosy where she had a shag. Little wonder that the barman, who actually didn't know who his father was, lost his rag, and wanted to punch Marky into next March. But he settled for throwing him out of the door. His victim landed on his head, so the barman phoned for an ambulance, but by the time it arrived Marky was long gone. He was en route to the next drinking emporium, having bought a woollen hat from a charity shop to staunch the blood as he went.

In Mooley's Pool Emporium he was struck by a cue, wielded by a man who hated Marky for reasons understandable enough. Marky had stolen his woman and the image of Marky shelfing her kept the guy awake every single night. By a fluke he hit Marky just where the blood from the earlier blow was congealing into a paste. It started flowing ever so freely again. No one was sympathetic because Marky had caused enough trouble in the pool hall in the past, especially playing for money and never coughing up the sovs when he lost. In Mooley's this was worse than murder, so he was a pariah and no one really cared about the red stuff that was pouring out of his head. This was a place where hustling was a job and people expected to be paid.

Then a new witness appeared, and what a witness! Taxi driver Marvin Gaye, yes that was it, got up from his seat. He was as fat a man as many had ever set eyes on. When he worked in the Turkish kebab place on Routher Lane there was so much of him going spare that wherever he stood in the kitchen inevitably some obese part of him was under the grill. Unlike the Motown singer this Marvin was white and could neither 'Get It On' nor perform 'Sexual Healing' on anyone, unless they were desperate beyond. He flabbed his way forward, all twenty-nine stone of him, parts of him rippling even when he was standing stock-still. As he sat down the chair gave way beneath him, and the people in court could barely stifle their laughter as the legs splayed out beneath his mighty weight. Even the coroner looked as if he was really holding himself in check.

Once everyone had regained their composure, and the court itself had found a sturdy-looking metal chair for Marvin, he described an altercation between Marky and a man who had yet to be traced by the police. Marky had apparently mocked the man's religious T-shirt, which said *I believe in Marina* and had told him unequivocally that Marina was a whore. The man had swung for him.

216

Although the punch hadn't connected, Marky had fallen backwards – no doubt due to the amount of alcohol he'd ingested that day. His head had struck the pavement with an audible crack as he fell. Even then he had managed to get back on to his feet to curse the man, who was offering him a hand-up, but he did gather up the various cartons from Bangalore Delite which had emptied out of a plastic bag. Marky got into Marvin's cab in a daze. He talked all the way home but Marvin couldn't figure out a word he said and, yes, he answered the coroner, he might well have been concussed.

When they arrived at their destination Marvin had watched the drunk man stagger up the front garden path in an action that resembled a slalom in slow motion. He had fallen again against the post of the washing line but had once again picked himself up, as if this was always the way, the most natural thing in the world. He had crashed against a wooden fence but had managed to turn back to face Marvin as he put the key in the door, marvelling at his own ability and giving a defiant salute in the vague direction of the taxi. It had been quite a show.

Marvin was thanked for his evidence and then they called Marky's wife Poppaline. There was a slight hiatus, as she was outside smoking a spliff to calm her nerves.

She was asked about what happened after Marky came into the house. Poppaline explained that he had started to put plates on the table, had gone as far as to start peeling the lids off containers, when he'd announced that he was going upstairs for a slash, as he put it. She'd then heard him falling down the stairs and when she went to look he was lying on his back in the hallway having difficulty breathing.

'What did you do then, Mrs Divotts?'

'I stroked his earlobes, m'lud.'

'His earlobes?'

'I'd read in a magazine that that was what you did.'

'I see. And I take it this wasn't *The Lancet*.'

Poppaline didn't get the joke, and the coroner was surprised with himself for saying such a thing.

'I rubbed them very hard as he wasn't breathing.'

'And then?'

'I called an ambulance.'

There had been cackles of laughter in court and the coroner paused a little while before questioning her further. There was a bit of to-ing and fro-ing as he tried to match up the timings as she described them with the official log from the Ambulance Service. Then he twigged.

'And what happened to the chicken dansak, Mrs Divotts?'

'I ate it. No point in good food going to waste.'

The coroner didn't argue with her, but did clarify that she had in fact eaten the Indian takeaway before ringing 999.

'So you ate the food while your husband was lying there, possibly fighting for his life?'

'I did.'

There was a dumbstruck silence. They would never know which blow was the fatal one, but most of those present would remember Marvin's description of the skull hitting the pavement after the altercation with the Marina

218

fan. The local paper made much play of this episode in the drunken saga. They had listed the items Marky had purchased, which his wife had promptly consumed as he lay there. Keema nan. King prawn puri. Chicken tikka masala. One portion of pilau rice. Three popadums. While he drew his last breaths.

Wednesday's post brought with it an invitation to appear on the *Best Enterprise* programme to talk about his business and its successes. Strimmer hadn't actually heard of the show but they said there'd be a fee and transport would be arranged, which all sounded fair enough. He was asked to ring one of the researchers, Becky or Rhiannon, who would ask him a few questions by way of background detail and make all the necessary arrangements.

The car that picked him up was in the very swanky category and now that he was living in a new bayside apartment it seemed more than appropriate. He had extensive views over the acres of dead water impounded behind the barrage, stretching all the way to Penarth Head. At night when he had the curtains drawn he projected an image of the view onto his enormous plasma screen TV. He liked the irony.

Anyone who remembers quality current affairs programmes, anything from *Newsnight* to *Sixty Minutes*, would wince at the production values of *Best Enterprise*, which replaced veracity with mendacity. To begin with there was the small matter of the producers using subterfuge and out-and-out deceit to lure their guests onto the show. Then there was the fact that the programe staff colluded so freely with the police – lending them tapes, buying information, a two-way traffic that was condoned by pretty much everyone. In the Golden Age they simply wouldn't have done it. But then again that was the day of the programme: this was the age of the show.

The set looked like a cocktail lounge and programme staff did, indeed, serve cocktails to the studio audience. There were dayglo sofas and a generally retro feel to the set design, with big globe lights and zebra stripes much in evidence.

There were also stand-up comics to warm up the audience and live bands out to promote whatever single they happened to be touting at that moment. When they got round to pillorying the guests it was of a piece with the rest of the show, both in tone and register.

One of tonight's bands was a raw rap band that might draw fair comparison with The Coup, while the other, Smiley's Yards, was part of the resurgence of interest in traditional folk singing. Then came a close-to-the-bone comedian whose material evoked more than distant echoes of the late Chubby Brown: scabrous and racy, he took no prisoners, showed no mercy. He also managed to make some swear words seem fresh, though, which was no mean feat.

It was time for Strimmer to make his appearance. He was feeling relaxed after a long chat with the make-up lady and two Purple Hazes, cocktails made with alcohol and powdered beta blockers, obtained on the black market by one of the research team. The make-up lady was, in fact the producer, who found this disguise a useful way of gauging the nervousness of the guests. She was also able to glean many a tasty titbit in the minutes it took her to apply the powder, banish the rings round the eyes, obliterating wrinkles. Strimmer seemed to be taking it all in his stride: in any case, the bouncers could sort things out if he did go off on one. She recalled a guy a couple of months back who hadn't been frisked on the way in. He ran amok with a pair or rice flails, making the boy band on set scatter like hares.

'Nail him,' said Lucrezia to the presenter in his earpiece when she had got to her seat in the vision gallery. She knew that the secret films of Strimmer they had to hand were dynamite, especially as they were so bloody and gory, showreeling a whole sequence of animals being eviscerated. They had made sure that the footage made it as clear as can be that not all of the animals were dead exactly when they were being skinned. It would have to follow a warning to viewers, which was usually a guarantee of a larger audience in itself. They also had a gentler, more pastoral film, with lots of breezy music which showed Strimmer catching squirrels in Ynysybwl. She liked the way they'd used a lot of Sixties music, the Youngbloods, Donovan and Jefferson Airplane. and given the material a sepia wash. That came first.

As Strimmer walked on to a great burst of applause the show's presenter Zammy Starstruck was waltzing around in front of the audience with one of his other guests in time to the theme tune. His dancing partner was a B-list Welsh actress who had found fame late in life as the star of porno films made by and for old age pensioners. They were tame but entertaining, and were funded by the government as a way of getting men to check their testicles, a message that was underlined by clunky lines of dialogue in officialese, spoken by old ladies in negligees and open-crotch pantaloons.

Zammy thanked Elsie and walked straight over to Strimmer but this time, unlike the way things had gone in rehearsals, he took him over to a small kitchen area rather than onto one of the extremely comfortable sofas. There stood a man with an improbably hefty stomach, dressed in chef's whites, as if ready to cook them something delicious. He sharpened a Sabatier knife even as Zammy ran through the scripted introduction, which he read off the autocue on Camera 3.

'We might be able to describe you as a man of mercurial talent and a rare gift for business whose rise to the top has been at the speed of a comet and all this without ever properly registering a company.'

A trap made of words. Strimmer sensed that things had taken a turn for the worse because the band had changed from playing a jaunty undertow to the conversation to something more strident. He felt metal jaws closing in on him, steel dentition able to break his back with a snap. There had also been a lighting change, so the set was now like a noir movie, all black and white and washes of dove grey. It was dramatic. He most certainly didn't like being one of the dramatis personae.

'Because we've been to Companies House, and there isn't a single record of any of the company names under which you trade. Likewise, the taxman has no record of you paying any tax whatsoever, which is about as serious a crime as you can commit in this country. We looked under 'Taste Bud Teasing', we looked under your full name, we looked under your alias, and it was like looking for someone who didn't exist. Which suggests something fishy, or someone with something to hide.'

Strimmer could feel the sweat running in rivulets through the cake of make-up. Some of it ran into his eyes. It stang.

'Are you feeling a little uncomfortable? Do you have an urge to run away? Wait awhile, there's plenty more to come.'

They screened the film of Strimmer preparing a St David's Day meal for Tre-coed school, busy as an ant in the unit on the estate. At one stage an enormous bloated rat made a bid for freedom. Strimmer was seen chasing after it with a cleaver, in a scene redolent of the Keystone Kops, but any urge to laugh was stifled by the graphic terror that followed, as slaughter ensued and the pans on the stove started simmering. He added leeks to the water after skinning the huge rat which must have been the size of a bobcat, a rat and a half. Lots of leeks floated in crimson water. It was for St David's Day, after all.

Strimmer was rooted to the spot, as his life was dismantled before his eyes. He thought for an instant of a greenfinch caught by his grandfather using bird lime, the tiny twig-like legs glued to a tree. The band struck up with the Boomtown Rats' 'Rat Trap' and the audience were encouraged to join in with the lines *It's a rat trap honey, and you've been caught.* Apposite. Catchy.

The cameras homed in on the chef now, as he had just

finished cooking and was sprinkling coriander on the plates. An actor dressed up as a butler, complete with white gloves, placed plates on a tray and took them to the dining table, which Strimmer hadn't noticed before.

'Would you care for some Brecon Carreg, the sparkling water that refreshes the palate?' asked the gushing presenter, working his way up to the annihilation. He looked deep into the camera lens, establishing a bonhomie with the viewer.

'Our chef here, Boris, has been recreating one of your favourite recipes, at least I think it's one of your favourites, as you seem to be awfully fond of serving it up to all and sundry. Boris isn't really sure whether he's cooked it long enough, though, and goodness only knows where it's been. Do you know where it's been Boris?'

Boris grunted.

'Don't mind him, Strimmer. He's from one of those former Soviet Republics you've never heard of. Lotsofoilistan or wherever. Great cook, though. Used to work at the Dorchester. Three Michelin stars, though you have to ask how anyone who can't speak a word of English manages to communicate with his staff? Must be genius, Boris? Boris?'

Boris nodded again, pretending, as always, not to understand a word.

'Maybe you'd like to take us through the array of flavours that envelop the tongue with this one. I think you'd call it a fricassee?'

Strimmer grudgingly picked up a spoon and scooped up a mouthful off the plate. There seemed to be an awful lot of teeth and jaws in the mix, as if they'd used more heads than they should have. It looked like the recipe he'd served up to the kids that time, but he couldn't really concentrate as his mind was racing through various permutations of the way this might turn out. He could see himself losing his flat and envisioned a time behind bars. He remembered how he'd once used a huge jar of garam masala to disguise the flavour of some condemned meat he bought on the cheap from someone who found it in a skip. That was one of his riskiest recipes, but luckily no one died as a consequence.

Strimmer couldn't face the food, as its smell was overpowering, so when he threw up over Zammy in quite the most spectacular case of projectile vomiting the awestruck vision mixer in the gallery had ever seen, it was no surprise to Strimmer, whose stomach had given him the thirty-second warning but for Zammy, well, this was the moment his luck turned. The freeze frame of him covered in the contents of someone else's stomach, his hair lank with such a volume of gastric juices that it seemed to be plastered to his skull, became the defining image of his career. Or end of it. He would never again be able to strike a suave posture, as people would always remember him this way. It was like the moment a politician loses his footing on the beach and the photo of him stumbling becomes the visual metaphor for his lack of control, for things slipping away from him.

Lucrezia's sides hurt from laughing. Similarly, her colleagues in the gallery were in convulsions. Camera 2 was all wobbly as the operator laughed hysterically. But then a phone call came through which forced them all to gather their wits about them. Within seconds they were interrupting their broadcast to flash up a breaking news story full of pictures of Marina, intercut with archive footage of the paper boat being found in California. The studio audience, and the crew in the production gallery, were mesmerized by pictures of a young man looking bashful and nervous under all the lights, cameras flashing fit to trigger epilepsy. Argentina, and a boy who collected waste paper for a living who had been tracked down by a reporter, Kent Lachan, who had decamped to Buenos Aires all those years ago and had finally got the root of the story, and got himself the sort of scoop that Citizen Kane would have commended.

And then, as every TV set in the land tuned in, there were the pictures of her, an old black-and-white video of Flavia and her husband Hector dancing at someone's wedding, of the couple way, way back and it was one of the most tender and affecting bits of footage in the whole history of moving image, because the story the young man was recounting into the bank of cameras and microphones was so incredible, and the sense you got of the simple love between the man and woman was in its way frightening because you thought to yourself, of course their love was the sort that could transcend time, and of course she lived on beyond him because of his prayers and pure desire to see her somewhere in the afterlife.

It was a happy accident, a Hollywood style happenstance, that all this occured on the day that Wales voted to

226

officially embrace the new religion, even though its theology was riddled and ragged and so much of its artifice was clear as daylight, but now they knew who she was, and it helped in deciding what to do with her as she continued to travel a world which was her limbo. It was time to bury her, with dignity. In Horacio's grave, of course.

The studio audience were glued to their seats, wanting to see the pictures again, to hear more about Flavia and her tango dancing and see the house where she lived, which will be an Argentine National Monument by the end of the week. The tourists flocking there to see it will make the whole country rich and it will rival even Brazil's economy in a couple of years. No longer is it just another South American country with a proud nation but it's also Marina's birthplace, and so they have a New Jerusalem on the River Plate.

When the studio was eventually cleared Lucrezia offered to buy both Strimmer and Zammy a drink, knowing that something changed this evening, love came to conquer capitalism and greed maybe, something big anyway. The love of an old man which was sufficient to keep a small craft safe in open waters, to take his love drifting with it in its wake.

In the bar Strimmer smiled at the two television people who had tortured him on TV, bringing the bright shining edifice of his life crumbling down. He forgave them and as he did so a warm sensation flowed through him, like wetting his pants when he was a boy. He started to sip his Glenmorangie while waiting for the cops. Lucrezia looked into her presenter's eyes and told him not to worry: whatever happened she would be there for him and he was amazed, as this was the famous Teflon lady and she was looking at him as if she cared for him. So he smiled at her and she smiled back and they were in good company, as everyone was smiling and happiness was very much the order of the day, and it was as if everyone had had a toke of Poppaline's weed, which was a marijuana fit for space travel.

On every TV in the land the pictures of the graceful tango were repeated over and over and over again and no one tired of seeing them, the haughty heads, the intricate steps, the way he looked at her as they turned in an elegant arcs and hey, they did look as if they could dance for ever.

Remember the words of the old song, the one they never tired of hearing:

> *Una lagrima tuya*
> *Que moja el alma*
> *Mientras rueda la luna*
> *Por la montana.*
> *Yo no se si has llorado*
> *Sobre un panuelo*
> *Nombrandome*
> *Nombrandome.*
> *Con desonsuelo.*

> A tear from your eye
> Which is damp with the sadness of my soul
> As the moon passes
> Over the mountain.

I know now whether you
Cried into your handkerchief
While saying my name
While saying my name
In your sadness.

And in the flickering footage which informs every news bulletin, the old couple's steps seem to keep time with the pace of the crawler caption unrolling across the bottom of the screen, left to right. And to look at them you would have to say their faces were ablaze with love. Ablaze with it.

Every story is a love story: so said someone, once upon a time. And when you come to think about it, really come to think about it, it is true, and even the worst tragedy is about the possibility of future love being thwarted. A family's love dies in the motorway pile-up. A mother's love dies with the dessicated corpse of a baby in a parched African land. The worst thing in life is knowing you are going to be taken away from the ones you love, by age, by illness, by time.

Over the city tonight the sunset is tangerine ribbons and sauvignon grape. It's an autumn sun which likes to linger awhile, likes to dally over its leaving. Colour, time, light, all washed together into this moment. Which this trio – Lucrezia, her new paramour and recent victim – can savour through the low windows of Bar Cwtsh, as the parochial accountants and the minor politicians and the lovestruck teenagers from Wattstown and Troedyrhiw and all the others in the bar still hang on every word the anchor-woman says about the boat being taken to the river and then launched without ceremony or so much as a single word. They all sip their drinks meditatively as the mystery is diminished, dissipated almost.

In the old Lido on Barry Island that's been adapted into an enormous nightclub the Devil dances alone. Were it not for the stumpy candles he has ignited with his breath he would be dancing in the dark. He smells now, he's in need of a good wash, and his spirit has collapsed somewhat since finding out that the old woman was in fact no fit adversary. Who can he challenge now? Whose energy can he steal?

And somewhere an old couple dance to the strains of an old tune . . .

Every story is a love story.

No more. No less.

The water in the bay is shot with mandarin flakes of leftover light, which challenges dusk to smother it completely, but the twilight insinuates as it always does, forcing the gulls to settle to their roosts on Roath Park Lake and the edges of the river Rhymney.

Because the big ships no longer dock in Cardiff she will arrive in Milford Haven, after journeying from Port Accra and Bremen and Stockholm and Cadiz. There will be welcoming parties, of course, but they won't be the frenzied masses of before. But she is coming. Flavia. Marina. She is coming. But this time she will be prepared for her journey home. Wales will be her penultimate port of call.

They had built a temple for her stay, using a rare volcanic marble only found on one single isle off the Sardinian coast, and while she will still lie there, in state, in her state, the fact that she now has a birthdate and a social security number has robbed her of something ethereal. They were expecting tourists in great numbers but anyone who wants a true connection with her will go to South America. So the ships due to follow her never arrive. The country settles back into some sort of hibernation.

The last glimmer of sun works its way through the venetian blinds of the Travelodge near Culverhouse Cross, where Poppaline Divotts is counting the hairs on the back of a travelling salesman who sells cheap shoes. She can't sleep. Hasn't been able to since the inquest, which poisoned her with guilt. On the floor are eight pairs of fake Italian leather designer boots and shoes – made in Guangdong. She's been gifted them by the man with a hundred and thirteen hairs on his back. Some of the shoes fit.

She remembers how Marky used to make her laugh, especially when he did that trick with Sambuca, where he set fire to the liqueur in her mouth, then smiled at her as the blue flame spread across his lips. Sometimes, when he was feeling brave or foolhardy he would even let the burning liquid dribble down his chin so would have a beard of fire. He had to make damn sure he didn't inhale, mind. That way lay months in intensive care.

A hundred and fourteen. A hundred and fifteen. Shit, what a lot of hairs.

The dark settles in Rover Way and Treherbert Way, on Sandman's Close and Mystic Terrace. Eight thousand miles away a nun in her simple cell hears a knock on the door, quiet but insistent.

'Who's there?' she asks, in a voice hoary with sleep.

'God,' comes the reply, even though the voice bears more than a passing similarity to the gardener who works the grounds and has had his eyes on her for quite some time. Quite some time.

She waits a long while before answering. Being lonely is to be cold in the night.

She waits almost as long as Esmeralda, after Manuelito asks her to marry him, after ten years of courtship, on his knees in the Tres Estrellas with everyone staring at him. As he gets back on his feet she notices that way he has of moving, the muscles moving lithe and graceful. A cat indeed, a leopard or jaguar, full of stealth and power. 'El Gato'. How beautifully appropriate. And man is an animal, like it or not.

In Malibu an actor who first spoke the sacred texts is taking stock of his life and absorbing the news about Flavia. He gives his new wife an energetic kiss using a mouth that's just been insured for ten million dollars. He will give her a billion dollars' worth of kisses in a weekend. She closes her eyes, humming with pleasure.

And behind him in the mirror, where the Devil is trimming his eyebrows which have run wild like vines, he can see a couple that has just entered the Lido through a hole in the fence to get some privacy and they are osculating like mad, as if their kisses are driving them insane, this television presenter and his producer and he can see the old pattern re-emerging. The old rhythm, the quotidian round. Name. *Ka*. *Ba*. Heart. Shadow. He remembers his time in Egypt, back in the good old days when there were resourceful deities to challenge, and plenty of gold to use as bait when it came to claiming souls.

On board a ship heading for the Pembrokeshire coast two members of the Pink Berets, Jim Martinez from Pensacola, Florida and Duane Michael Carter from Cable, Illinois, are falling for each other even as they stand sentry over Marina on her plinth. On this her last but one voyage. And Jim swears to this day he saw her winking at him, not once but twice, even as Dwayne crabbed sideways ever so discreetly, eyes straight forward, to be a little nearer to him.

Marina stayed in Wales for a week, then, in a touching ceremony involving a massed choir with children from every school in the land, she headed off to Buenos Aires, a woman now, not a God, even though the cults would not disband, and it would take decades to unpick the strands of new theology that had gathered around her.

And that might have been that were it not for the shrines that started to appear.

On a lane near Penmon Priory on the isle of Anglesey a model house was erected overnight, not more than twelve inches high, but inside there was a miniature, framed photograph of Flavia as she danced. Looking out at the oil rigs of Liverpool Bay, the little candle that lit the house's interior stayed alight despite any wind that blew. That was beyond science, in itself.

In Llanddewi Brefi, in the green undulating hills of Ceredigion, a wooden shrine just appeared one night, in a lay-by where the council stores salt and grit to spread on roads in the winter. It sported fluttering purple banners, and over the weeks someone left a brand new pair of high-heeled wooden shoes, a pack of cigarettes, a half bottle of Torrontés wine, all manner of little offerings, and there were always fresh flowers, and you would often find one of the cigarettes burning in a holder as if someone had just left. Not that you'd ever see them. As if invisible folk placed them in the shrines. Next to the posies of flowers – bright gentians, speedwells and flowering heads of centaury.

The shrines grew by accretion, as if several hands were at work on each one. A shrine full of snowdrops near Dafydd ap Gwilym's grave at the Cistercian abbey at Strata Florida. Another, made of shards of slate, on empty moorland near Cwm Heskyn, land of merlin and grouse, pipit and ousel. Three at equal intervals on a path in Pembrokeshire, the purple pennants always flickering in the onshore breeze.

Soon these shrines were plentiful yet you never saw anyone putting them there, or placing anything in them.

The shrines punctuated long lengths of motorway, and could sometimes stand six feet tall, but smaller ones were also located at leafy junctions on roads less travelled. On limestone ridge and above the coal measures, near kissing gates and on elm avenues. Even on the remotest rocks, such as South Bishop, where the only person who could have built the little cairn that stood above the puffin burrows would have been the Trinity House engineer, there to inspect the lighthouse. A blossoming of shrines, an innocent rash of them.

From Moelfre to Cwmrhydyceirw, from Garnswllt to Penmaenmawr, little shrines, mushrooming, in all their frail and fragile architectures. Someone would clean them, someone would leave pictures of the family to be blessed.

These honest and simple temples: giving expression, or candlelight hope to travellers, who would sometimes pause contemplatively, thinking of an old lady from a country far away and what she meant to them. They might then nod briefly, pensive but satisfied, before walking on with renewed vigour.

Acknowledgements

Thanks to Ceri, Mairwen and Lowri and all the staff at Gomer for their warm support, and to Francesca Rhydderch for proofreading and making a great many insightful suggestions. *Diolch o waelod calon i chi gyd.*

Adapting my Welsh-language novel *Dala'r Llanw* as *Uncharted* was one of many things I was able to do as the recipient of a Creative Wales award from the Arts Council of Wales. Huge thanks, therefore.

Jason Wilson's *Buenos Aires: A Cultural History* was an invaluable source as was www.planet-tango.com which is clearly a labour of love and gratefully acknowledged.

Acknowledgements